*NOTE: this novel is free of AI generated or revised content.
No portion was written, edited, or enhanced through the use of AI.*

- JJ Renck

Cover Design – Jaycee DeLorenzo
Publishing Coordinator – Sharon Kizziah-Holmes

,

I0566411

Published by

LAKEPOINT PRESS LLC®

Paperback ISBN 13: 979-8-9905504-9-0
Hardcover ISBN 13: 979-8-9988175-0-2
eBook ISBN 13: 979-8-9988175-1-9

For Steve
and all the diligent physicians and nurses
who labor with compassion for those requiring
long-term acute care.

proscribe: *v.tr.* reject or denounce (a practice, etc.) as dangerous; proscription *n.*

- *Oxford English Reference Dictionary, 2nd edition, 1996, p. 1159*

ONE

October 10th

Thursday

She hated having a throng at these things. The expanding crowd made it hard to think. She stood at the foot of the bed, totally focused on the object of their intense efforts, a man in his sixties. He had suffered more complications than one individual should have to endure in a lifetime. This needed to end, and soon.

"Okay, let's give one more dose of epi, then that'll have to do it," Dr. Erica Lange ordered.

The nurse's head snapped up. She threw the doctor a sharp look, not missing a beat with her vigorous chest compressions. "Has it been long enough?"

Another pair of eyes, those of the respiratory therapist, stared at the doctor as well, while continuing to deliver Ambu bag generated breaths on cue – manual ventilation being delivered through a re-established endotracheal tube.

"Continue the compressions for five more minutes. Are you tired? Do you need relief?"

"No, I'm good, but—"

1

"This is a hopeless case, and never should have been a full code, anyway," Dr. Lange interrupted. "We've done all we can." The nurse gazed down at the lifeless man – a man she'd cared for over the past five weeks – and continued her role in the resuscitation. Behind her, Erica heard hallway noises through a now-open door, rustling and whispers, then a gasp. She turned slightly and saw the patient's wife and daughter standing just inside the door.

"Oh, my God, why would you say that?" the younger woman asked, her audible anxiety hidden from no one. The man's wife stared, stricken and rendered mute.

Erica motioned to a nurse at her left elbow to attend to the family members who slid away to inform and comfort them. Focusing again on the patient, Erica heard murmuring about stepping out, but they refused to leave the room.

She drew herself up to all of her five-foot, six-inch frame and braced for the confrontation which would follow. There had been no reasoning with this family over the past several weeks, especially as his clinical condition spiraled downward, organ systems failing one after the other. Now, at the final eclipse, they weren't going to take it well. That was obvious. And she expected a showdown with some of the nursing staff, to boot.

"Okay, let's call it. Please stop."

"No, no," the daughter wailed, pushing through the gathered personnel, throwing herself across her father's still body. "It can't be, can't be," she cried out. Erica placed a hand on her shoulder, but the young woman pushed her hand away and screamed, "Don't touch me! You did this. You wanted this all along!"

It was time to take hold. Erica didn't respond to the daughter's outburst or charges, and backed away as the man's wife joined her distraught daughter at the bedside. She motioned for the team to pack up the intrusive resuscitative equipment and exit the room with her, save one nurse who remained with the family.

"Take this out!" the daughter demanded, reaching for the

endotracheal tube firmly positioned in her father's throat. The attending nurse arrested her hand midair, and gently explained it had to remain in until it was officially removed in the morgue. Pulling it then, with the cuff inflated, would have been another bad moment, considering his fragile clotting status, and the resultant blood running from his mouth – not a good sight. The nurse's swift intervention elicited additional moans and expletives from the bereaved young woman.

Her mother sat mute, staring at her deceased husband. The road had ended there, in the long-term acute care facility. A place where he had planned to recover fully, and from which he would have ventured forth to resume his normal life.

At least that was what they had been led to expect.

Two

He regretted agreeing to this plan, but it was necessary, or so he'd been told. Director of Nursing, Richard – Ric – Newman wished this task had fallen onto someone else's shoulders. He loved his new position, had waited a good while to attain it, but this 'duty' was burdensome. Why didn't Dr. Lange just stop her darn crusading? Managing his thoughts, he staked out a spot at the main nursing desk and kept watch. It was the most important task he had to complete right then, anyway.

When Dr. Todd Griswold emerged from a room and washed his hands, Ric seized the moment and strode toward him. "Dr. Griswold, may I have a word?"

The harried internist looked up from the sink, regarded the nurse, and asked, "What about?"

"I'd rather we discuss it in my office, if you don't mind."

Without questioning further, the doctor jerked paper towels from the dispenser, saying only, "All right," and turned on his heel. Having received tacit agreement to a discussion, Ric led the way to his cramped office, just off the nursing station. All eyes followed the two as they made their

4

way into the Director of Nursing office. Ric shut the door firmly behind them and paused.

"Have a…"

But the busy doctor, dispensing with formalities, had already taken a chair in front of Ric's desk, and leaned forward on the arm rests, apparently impatient for the talk to be initiated and concluded. "So, what's the issue we couldn't discuss in the hall?"

"I'll be frank—"

"Please do."

"So, we had a code late this morning on Mr. Franklin, and it didn't go so well."

"We expected he would have trouble—"

"Correct, but Dr. Lange conducted it, and the family got upset."

"Which isn't a surprise."

"No, but they overheard her saying that it was a hopeless case and he shouldn't have been a full code anyway."

"Why was the family even in the room during that?"

"No one saw them approach and didn't intervene before they could get in the room."

"Okay, go on."

"And several of the nurses present think she called the code too soon, didn't give Franklin a chance to pull through."

Dr. Griswold stared at Ric. "Were you there?"

"Only at the very end. I was detained upstairs in my main office, tied up on the phone when it was announced. I knew there was plenty of staff to handle it."

"Okay, I'll take care of it, and talk with her."

"Dr. Griswold, this is happening too much. She seems to be on some sort of campaign, always trying to get do-not-resuscitate orders out of patients. Some families have complained to the nurses that they feel pressured. That they assumed they didn't come here to die."

"I said, I'll take care of it." Griswold stood from the chair and took the three short steps toward the door. Turning back, he said, "You know it's not improper to inquire of

5

patients what their advanced plans are. There's a policy requiring you all to do that."

"Of course. I understand that. But Ms. Nelson specifically told me to let you know if Dr. Lange kept it up."

"And you've let me know. I'll speak with Kristine Nelson. I need to finish rounds now."

With that he left the confines of the small office, and strode through the nursing station, fewer eyes following his exit than his entrance.

Ric, seated at the small metal desk, stared across the beige room at a nondescript landscape print which was intended to brighten the windowless space and its bland décor, as well as engender pleasant thoughts and a positive attitude in whichever Director of Nursing currently occupied the space. It failed in that assignment, and the god-awful fluorescent lights offered the artwork no favor, and only augmented Ric's threatening headache.

Still anxious, he mindlessly tidied the few papers strewn there. This was not a good situation, one which he now suspected he should have avoided. But he'd follow the rules, even if they were a little too fluid for his liking, and keep this position. He had a fiancé now who wouldn't understand him walking away from such a good position, especially over some doctor's behavior. They had big plans, after all.

~ ~ ~ ~

Having finished his exam, Dr. Griswold straightened from leaning over the woman's bed. She'd made progress, though, more than several subspecialists had predicted. Confident he could give the family a fairly good report, he glanced out the adjacent window, appreciating the setting sun and the brilliant horizon. It was about time to wind it up for the day, but he had one more duty to attend to. And with most other doctors and day staff gone, he could perform the assessment without anyone really wondering what he was doing.

With one last glance at the dozing woman, he left the room, washed his hands, and made his way down the hall. He knew which patients Dr. Lange had seen that day, other than Mr. Franklin who had coded, so he'd start at the other end. As a matter of fact, he'd probably already compiled enough information – damning information – on her activities to move forward as planned.

He hurried to the first patient's room, unlocked the pulldown desk outside the door, and signed on to the computer terminal there. After all, being the head of the internal medicine group he could survey any chart he wished. No one would think it out of order for him to check on one of his partner's patients. It just wasn't done that often, unless they were on call for an evening or weekend. But, who's going to say anything? Who's going to report him? No need to worry.

He tapped in his password and stared at the screen. Pulling up the progress notes, he quickly found Dr. Lange's entries for that week. Yup, there it was – her charted entry regarding resuscitation counseling. Mentioned several times that week, in fact. Griswold closed out that chart; he'd seen all he needed to and moved on to the next door. This whole crusade of hers had to stop. And soon.

"Oh, Dr. Griswold, you're still here," came a voice from his right.

He glanced up, threw the nurse a smile, and said, "You're right."

"Can I help with anything? You probably want to get out of here."

"I'll be done in a few minutes, but thanks, anyway."

He ended the exchange by turning again to the computerized chart and Erica's note from that day. The nurse moved effortlessly down the hall, her cushioned shoes squishing with each step.

And there it was again. End-of-life counseling filled more space than other clinical observations of that day.

Yes, he knew exactly what he had to do.

7

THREE

Friday

Having completed his rounds, Dr. Grant Ashton Meyers – Ash, to those close to him – laid a hand on the door knob and immediately knew someone was in their designated office. An upset someone. Emotional noises rose from within. The small space allotted to the subspecialists, who attended at Oakwood Specialty Hospital, was on the second-floor mezzanine and out of the way, used only to finish dictations or other paperwork, undisturbed. Besides, he needed to retrieve a couple of reports he'd left there, as well as his jacket, and get over to his office. Several patients had already checked in and were waiting, his nurse had informed him.

Unsettling sounds rose again from the interior, but he turned the handle anyway.

Obviously surprised at the unexpected intrusion, the nurse practitioner Raina Crawford stared at him, and he stared back. She maintained a comforting hand on Dr. Erica Lange's shoulder, who sat hunched over, sobbing. He paused, glanced over his shoulder to check whether anyone in the hall might have noticed the scene, then stepped into the office and

8

closed the door.

"What's the problem here?"

Erica looked up, her cheeks tear-streaked, and wiping her face, attempted a faint smile. It wasn't convincing. Raina patted her shoulder, but offered no explanation.

Dr. Meyers rephrased his inquiry. "Has something happened?"

"You could say that," Erica answered.

"Do I need to know about it?"

His jacket hung on the back of the chair, and his papers were pinned under her elbows, fixed in place. He'd have to dislocate her, or wait. He wisely opted for the latter.

"I'd like you to know."

Assuming the only available other chair, he said nothing and waited. Obviously, she was overwrought, and this conversation was not going to be dispatched quickly. He'd always considered her a composed professional, at least during the clinical contacts they'd shared. Well put together and certainly stunning.

Usually pulled back or secured upward, her raven hair now hung around her face and shoulders as if unleashed from its confines by her sudden emotional melt down. Her large black eyes, now fixed on him, conveyed anger, hurt, and some fear. And then he noted her mascara sufficiently smudged to likely require removal or repair before she saw any more patients. He'd learned from his wife that messed up mascara was not a good look. But, beyond that, he had no idea how a woman would go about fixing such a situation.

Her voice halting, Erica launched into the summary of what brought her to that point. "They got all over my case after Mr. Franklin coded yesterday."

"Who's they?"

"Dr. Griswold and Kristine Nelson. And Ric Newman."

He nodded.

She went on, "Said I, or we, are supposed to go through the case manager if we want to get a DNR on a patient. That we can't just run around talking with patients or families

9

without them being present. The social worker or the Director of Nursing. It's against policy."

Raina gave Erica's shoulder a gentle rub and frowned at Ash.

Wait a minute...was this his fault? He wasn't sure where they placed him in this overall scenario. Perhaps he was viewed as a Griswold and Nelson sympathizer? After a moment's consideration, he decided to withhold his opinion for the time being.

"So, apparently the nurses, or at least several of them, are spying on me, checking to see who I talk to and reporting it to the charge nurse. Then apparently the charge nurse lets Ric Newman know. He must be keeping track."

On a roll then, her observations and complaints poured forth. "All I know is I've been here all of four months and they've made my life hell. It's ridiculous...all these patients are full codes unless they specifically speak up and want to discuss it with us. Even if they come with a form already completed for no resuscitation, most of the nurses go in and question them repeatedly about whether they wish to remain so. They badger them."

She gulped back sobs, and went on, "And then when I initiate a discussion with a patient or family, all hell breaks loose. I'm told I can't do that, and that patients and some families have complained about me bringing it up."

Sniffles and sobs took over, and she paused to wipe her eyes and face.

Well, this is not a quick discussion. Lots of material here to dissect. Ash took the opportunity then to break in with a few clarifying questions.

"So, this has been going on the whole time you've been in the medicine group?"

Erica nodded. "It seems like it."

"What did Griswold tell you when you signed on? Did he go over any of the policies?"

"Just a few. But, I don't recall him saying we had to clear such discussions with any nurse or a case manager.

10

That's just wrong. Many of these patients undergo futile, unnecessary resuscitations."

Now the conversation was veering toward familiar-sounding territory. Ash had heard rumors off and on that some patients had been made 'no code' against their will. But passing through the halls or while lingering near the main nursing station, he hadn't wished to engage the nurses when he overheard bits and pieces of such conversations. No one had ever told him to avoid appropriate discussions with various patients. And no one in his subspecialty intensivist group had said a thing about such an initiative, or about being cautioned or chastised.

"Sounds like you believe these are inappropriate procedures." He wasn't really wanting to frame it as a question. It was time to let her recover, recompose herself, and he needed to move on. Besides, if this was all true, then more investigation might be warranted. And he couldn't accomplish that today. He prepared to ask one last clarifying question when she spoke.

"Yes, I think those efforts are futile."

"All of the time?"

"Most...most of the time." She threw her head back and gave him a defiant look.

"Are you saying, then, that administration is interfering with independent medical decision-making? Are you going that far?"

"Yes, I do think that. Don't you?"

He couldn't say what he really thought at the moment. Nurses spying on her? Was this a reliable story? That was, in his mind, a bit of a stretch. But how could he know for sure? Maybe she was right.

"Well, I do think that's wrong, if that's the case, but I don't think we can solve this problem right now. How many more patients do you have to see today?"

"About four."

"Why don't you finish all that, and then speak with Griswold again tomorrow? Maybe if you talk with him after hours the conversation will seem less pressured."

He rose, and moved toward the desk, signaling his impending departure. It was well past time to retrieve his jacket and paperwork and head over to the office. He had ignored several pages from his nurse during this whole drama. It was time to get going. Raina stepped aside, allowing him room.

As he came alongside the desk chair, Erica apparently anticipated he might offer his hand, and grabbed his, clutching it longer than necessary. "I'm sorry to bother you with all this, really, but thank you. You're kind to listen to a blubbering woman." After a few moments, she released his hand.

"No problem. It will probably work out better than you think. Excuse me, my jacket," he explained, reaching behind her. He then eased his papers from under her forearms.

Erica seemed oblivious to being in the way. "I seriously doubt that." She mustered a faint smile.

He nodded and turned toward the door, feeling the need to say something a bit more reassuring.

"Well, let me know what happens."

"You can be sure I will."

In the hall then, the door closed behind him, he made his way toward the staircase. What a scene. Where would all this lead?

He had a sinking sensation he hadn't heard the last of it.

FOUR

Sunday

It was a beautiful evening, just cool enough to remind him that Indian summer had finally fled and full-on autumn had arrived. What a great time to linger outside or have dinner on the deck, both of which he intended to enjoy. It had been a busy week, and he had relished their time at home that weekend.

"Can you grab that bottle of wine, Margo, when you come out?"

"Be out in a minute," she called back.

He scooted the steaks from the flame, closer to the roasted potatoes, and turned off the grill. Their Golden Retriever Roberta, stretched out on the terrace, raised her head to assess the meal possibilities and alerted to the nightly flyover. A small flock of Canada Geese passed overhead, one of them honking signals, their wings emitting a low whirring noise with each rhythmic flap. An amazing sound, really. Ash and Roberta watched as they made their way to a nearby lake, and gracefully descended. As accustomed to it as he was, he often took note of the nightly flight ritual. You could practically set your clock to their regular evening

13

translocation.

The slider swished open. Margo emerged, toting the wine bottle under her arm, and a salad in her other hand. He relieved her of the bottle and poured two glasses waiting on the set table. Dinner was ready. Roberta rose and took her position beside the table, between the two of them, obviously hopeful for handouts.

"What a beautiful evening. Glad you suggested cooking out and enjoying the terrace." Margo patted Roberta's head as she sat down.

"Right. Before too long..." As he cut into his steak, Ash's phone vibrated with a call. "It'll get too cold to stay out here."

"Don't you need to check that? It may be one of the kids."

He smiled. "They'll keep for a few minutes. This steak might not." He glanced at the rare interior of the filet. "Just right. How's yours?"

Margo sipped her wine. "I don't need to look. I'm sure it's fine. Here's some salad."

Settled then, and curiosity prodding him, Ash picked up his phone and noted the missed call from an unfamiliar number. He'd wait until they finished dinner or until the other party cared to leave a voice message. If they didn't, then he'd not bother to respond. He wasn't on call duty that weekend, after all. Placing it beside him on the table top, he further ignored its intrusion.

Taking their time, he and Margo chatted about the change of seasons, upcoming holidays, and several landscaping projects in the works. Wondering how their two sons were faring at college that year occupied a good bit of the discussion. Had either of them heard from their sophomore son Clay, or the senior Cole? No, to Cole, of course. What college senior would hang on the phone with Mom and Dad, at least not frequently? But Clay had called Margo once to chit chat, and Ash on another occasion, asking for more money. Having verified that they were both equally informed of their sons' current situations, which they labeled as normal, they lapsed into thoughtful silence when Ash's phone chimed again with a message.

Pouring Margo more wine, he asked, "So, you leave tomorrow for Tulsa? That new client?"

"Right. I'll catch the early flight around eight. They've booked me through the week. It could spill over into Saturday, but we'll see."

"It sounds like an involved project. You plan to run back and forth?"

"For a while, but I may be able to handle quite a bit of it remotely once decisions are made and materials are ordered. It's an excellent new opportunity, which may lead to others, of course. A little hands-on never hurts."

Her burgeoning interior design business had taken off over the past couple of years, but now that the boys were out of the house, Ash found himself wanting more of her time, not less. And out-of-town clients really cut into their schedule. He hadn't discussed his feelings with her, wishing to avoid the appearance of a selfish, neglected male. Especially considering the burdens his own medical schedule had imposed on their marriage over many years. But why now, so many new remote clients? Couldn't one of her other associates go?

"How many buildings do they own?"

"Four. This is a new branch, but there are plans for expansion into two other cities over the next three years, I'm told. Should be interesting."

"So, who's covering the shop while you're away?"

"The other two."

"Isn't one of them going with you?"

"Not this time. There's too much work left over from summer. We got behind due to slowed shipping and need to wind that up before mid-November. The holidays coming and all."

Ash's phone chimed again.

Margo glanced at it rattling on the glass table top. "Don't

you need to check that?"

"I will, later. Got any dessert?"

"Sure. Let me take the dishes in and I'll get it. Why don't you attend to that call...at least see who's ringing you on a Sunday evening."

She slid from the table and made her way through the slider into their kitchen, Roberta on her heels. He heard her clattering around, preparing their dessert, and talking to the dog. It certainly had been a good weekend at home alone, relaxing, not racing around on errands or projects. Margo had been so efficient with her packing, he'd hardly noticed her time spent in trip preparations. Of course, keeping an eye on college football had proved a distraction.

He picked up his phone and dialed voice mail. Glad then he was holding it to his ear instead of broadcasting on speaker, there was one message, and the voice speaking to him was at the very least surprising, and not a little unsettling. He saved the message, disconnected, and stared into near space, not sure how to approach the required call back.

Interrupting his thoughts, Margo emerged again with a tray laden with apple pie dressed with ice cream for him, cheddar cheese for her, and decaf coffee for both. Her cooking always a treat, he wisely chose to suspend any further musings and enjoy what was offered. Perhaps the good old apple pie would clarify things for him.

"Who was that? Anything important?"

"It's hard to say."

Margo gave him a studied look, which he pretended to ignore. "It's hard to say who it was?"

"Whether it's important."

~ ~ ~ ~

"That's right, I was terminated yesterday. Given my walking orders."

"By whom? Griswold?"

"Right again."

"On a Saturday? That's a little odd."

"Well, I did what you suggested. Spoke with him, actually called him yesterday early afternoon."

Seated comfortably at their large desk, scanning his emails, Ash remained silent, gathering, or rather ordering, his thoughts. He gazed at his sleek laptop, then glanced around at the well-appointed room. Margo had made sure this room was warm and cozy, ready always to tuck in for reading or study, or quiet conversation. Books lined one wall of built-in shelves, tall curved windows stretched across the opposite expanse, allowing an unobstructed view to the east and the extent of their lawn, framed with tall evergreens, descending toward their nearest neighbor. Leather club chairs sat positioned for conversation. It was their little retreat, and he didn't want to sully his space with other people's freshly-hatched problems or controversies.

Erica took the opening, and launched into a reiteration of points she'd made on Friday. Emphasizing that various nurses were spying on her, reporting to the charge nurse whenever she spoke with a patient regarding code status, checking her charted progress notes – by Griswold, no less – and generally harassing her at every turn. She ran on until Ash had heard enough and jumped in.

"I can see where you're coming from, but I'm not sure what can be done about it. Have you spoken with Kristine Nelson?"

"Todd told me they had discussed the situation, and had agreed on the termination. I don't think I can gain anything by talking to her. He emphasized again that we are to go through the case manager when we wish to discuss advance directives with either a patient or family. That is the policy. Is that what your group does?"

"Can't say that it is. But usually you all in medicine have already established the code status, or it's on the chart by the time we become involved with the patient. I certainly haven't consulted with the case manager or the Director of Nursing before talking with patients about that. Or, any other clinical issue."

She cut in, "Besides, it's ultimately Griswold's decision whether I stay with the group. The Oakwood facility doesn't actually hire us individually. Our group is independently contracted with the corporation."

"I see. Has anyone else in your group had this problem?"

"Not that they've said. And now the other two are pretty closed-mouthed. Raina said she doesn't think they've been bothered, so far. But, I don't think they care about the issue, really. Not as much as I do."

"Well, look, Erica, I don't disagree with where you're coming from, but I don't see what I can do about this. Other than to clarify the policy which, if it exists, applies across the board. It's certainly concerning to me if they're inserting a case manager into medical decision-making. That isn't appropriate in my book, either."

"Right. You know, my basic position is a code should actually be a procedure the patient has to consent for, not be done automatically to them by default. Its success rate is miserable, taking all comers."

After considering her blunt – some would think crass – statement, he said, "That's an interesting position you take. It's not a wrong point, but we're not dealing with that reality right now. I do think, in the immediate term, we need to clarify with administration the issue of medical decision-making and the current policies."

"That's why I called, and I'm sorry to bother you on a Sunday evening…"

Rather than sounding annoyed with the intrusion, he suddenly felt something soothing was in order. "That's okay."

"So, I'm wondering if you could speak with Kristine Nelson and get her take on it. Is there anything she can do, or is willing to do, to reverse this? Or at least put it on hold, temporarily."

"I'm not sure."

"I know it's not your problem to solve, but I have to work. With two little kids, I can't just sit around waiting for something to clear up. I don't have someone else bringing in another paycheck for us."

Ash sat silent. He realized he knew nothing of her life situation, and frankly wasn't sure he wanted to. They were treading into the personal sphere, and he'd just as soon not go there. This conversation had taken a turn, one which he admittedly had dreaded.

She went on, "I don't know if you're aware of my divorce several years ago. My ex took off when I wouldn't move for his career. Truth was, he wasn't making the move entirely alone. So, I regrouped, left my first practice which was breaking up anyway, and thought Oakwood was a better option for me. Better hours, all that, with the kids. So, this is..."

Ash heard a choking sound as her voice trailed off. Better bring this discussion to a rapid conclusion if he could manage it, and end the call before Margo came in wondering what was keeping him. He didn't want this situation to occupy his thoughts the rest of their evening and into the night.

He let her compose herself, then said, "Look, Erica, you're under a lot of pressure. All I can do is speak with Kristine in a day or two. I'm not on Oakwood this week; I'm in the office. I can request an appointment and try to find out more details, but I can't promise anything."

Her voice sounding brighter, she said, "Oh, would you? I'm not expecting you to solve this, of course, but that gives me hope. At least you care enough to do something."

Whoa...care enough? "Frankly, I doubt I can reverse Griswold's decision."

"But, I appreciate you stepping in."

What had he just stepped into? "We'll see."

"I hope you'll get back to me fairly soon."

"I'll be in touch." They disconnected just as he heard Margo approach.

19

"Who was that, hon, someone from the group?"

"No, just someone I work with at Oakwood from time to time. They had a question." He rose from his desk and met her in the doorway, wrapping an arm around her slim waist.

"Not a problem, I hope?" She gave him a light peck on the cheek, and turned toward their bedroom.

"Yeah, hopefully not."

FIVE

Monday

Margo trudged through the back hall toward the mudroom, dragging an overloaded carryon. At the sound, Ash turned and looked up as she approached.

"I didn't think you were ready to go or I would have carried that out for you."

"I'm just bringing it this far. After I check a couple of emails, I'll be ready to leave."

He relieved her of the bag, loaded it into her car, and returned to find her in their study at the computer. Through the shutters, he could see the first brilliant red-hued streaks of dawn breaching the horizon. *Red sky in morning, sailor take warning...* Where on earth did that bothersome thought come from? Flushing the familiar verse, Ash focused on the view from their windows. The later sunrise, at the tail end of daylight savings time, always lent a too-early atmosphere to their morning routines, this day being no exception. Nonetheless, he was anxious to get to the office before the staff, and there to clear his desk after spending the previous week at Oakwood.

He stepped just inside the study door, seeking some sort

21

of satisfying goodbye before she departed. "Okay, it's loaded, and I'm off."

Margo looked up. "Sure. I'm about done here." She tapped a few more times, then closed out her business emails, and spun around. Standing then, she met him at the door. He wrapped her in a warm hug, lowered his head for a kiss. She returned his embrace, then pulled away and gave him a look.

A boyish grin decorating his face, he let her know, "I enjoyed last night."

"Um, me, too," she said, playfully assisting his turn toward the mudroom and back door. "We both need to move along and get out of here. You be good now. I hope your week goes well. I'll let you know when I arrive."

"Okay." At the door to the garage, he turned one last time, pecked her cheek, and finished with a gentle slap on her bottom.

"You go on," she ordered.

He smiled as he got in his large SUV, fired up the engine, and backed out of the garage. It had been a good weekend, and he looked forward to another in two weeks. But this week was busy for both of them going their separate ways, and with him on call that coming weekend, it was probably best she was preoccupied with the new client. Or the new client's entire new building. How she could look at a blank slate, literally just framed-in spaces, and create such striking interiors, he found amazing.

He smiled again as the neighborhood gates parted and he swung onto the busier street.

~ ~ ~ ~

"What exactly do you want to discuss, Dr. Meyers?" Kristine Nelson asked.

"Several issues which have come up recently." He glanced at his desk clock – 7:30 A.M. Margo should be boarding her flight.

"Issues?"

"Yes, concerning Dr. Lange."

"Oh, that."

Ash paused. Of course, he expected she would already know that Dr. Erica Lange had been relieved of her clinical duties with the internal medicine group. But, he suspected the sun had not even set Saturday evening before Kristine had been fully informed by Dr. Todd Griswold of the other doctor's sudden departure.

Why he didn't much care for the head of the internal medicine group he hadn't exactly settled in his mind, but the guy rubbed him the wrong way whenever he took his turn on call at Oakwood. Maybe it was Griswold's presumptuous manner, or his know-it-all attitude – when he obviously didn't have command of every subspecialty – that annoyed him. He knew he wasn't alone in his impressions. Several of Ash's pulmonary partners had commented that they couldn't trust Griswold to avoid doing something ill-advised on ventilator patients. Todd would then call at all hours of the night, wanting help with a situation gone bad. But, it was probably best to shelve his own relationship with Todd Griswold and attempt to address the basis of Erica Lange's swift departure. Perhaps, it hadn't been so swift after all.

He affirmed, "Yes, that. I'm not sure what you've been told, but I'd like to set an appointment sometime this week to discuss some things which have come to my attention since last Friday."

"Enough to know it was necessary," Kristine said in a rather flat tone.

He heard papers rustling on the other end and refrained from engaging the administrator in debate. In the background he also heard his own office back door opening and closing. The staff were arriving.

"How would tomorrow around eleven thirty work, just before lunch?" she suggested. "I have a thirty-minute slot then."

How nice it would be to have such a prescribed daily schedule that one could fit spur-of-the-moment people in like placing various pegs on a board. His office schedule on the other hand, at the end of most weeks, looked like somebody had bled red ink all over a bad English paper. Throw in time in the dialysis unit with unexpected work-ins there, ICU rounds, new consults, and well...his ability to flex seemed his strongest suit.

"Sure, I can make that work," he answered. He'd have to speak right away with his nurse, his chief scheduler – patient woman that she was – and rearrange several people. Or let no-shows solve the problem for him, though he couldn't count on that to create a convenient opening. This was important, and he'd given Erica his word he would at least attempt an appointment with Kristine Nelson.

They agreed quickly and disconnected. There. Done. Now it was time to get underway with the new week, and marginalize the old week's newest problem. He stepped through his office door.

"June? Did I hear you come in?"

Six

Tuesday

The office door swung open and the tall figure of a woman stood there. When Ash glanced up, he felt her intense gaze upon him. You couldn't help but notice her bright green eyes, a hue seldom seen. With her auburn hair backlit by the late morning sun streaming through her office windows, Kristine Nelson appeared almost rarefied. She then broke eye contact and spoke.

"Do come in." Backing away, she returned to her desk, taking a few moments to slide aside a small stack of papers. She turned her blinds downward, then made a show of checking her watch.

She wore a dark brown, almost black, tailored pantsuit, a pale yellow blouse, and minimal jewelry – a large-faced watch, silver earrings, and an impressive pale gemstone on her right middle finger. Minimal or not, her look exuded quality and money. Spoils of her not-so-recent divorce?

He took a chair in front of her desk, and tried to relax against the stiff back. He'd better get to it; the clock was running.

"I appreciate you meeting with me today."

25

"I'm sure you're busy, as well. You said you had become aware of issues with Dr. Lange." It was not a question.

"Yes, that's right. It came to my attention just the other day that she had been terminated from the internal medicine group. Matter of fact, I happened in on her and the nurse practitioner last Friday, and she was obviously upset at that time."

Only her fidgeting digits disrupted Kristine's perfectly still demeanor, and betrayed her pretense of calm as she gazed at him. A chink in the armor?

"Upset, you say?"

"Yes, obviously. Apparently, Ric Newman had just spoken with her about a code on Thursday. Several nurses had complained to him they thought she called it too soon. Didn't give the patient adequate opportunity to recover or respond."

"And you're concerned about her termination specifically because..."

"I've never noticed any problem with the quality of her patient care. And I understand that particular patient had PEA – pulseless electrical activity – which is a fatal situation. Codes don't usually solve that problem. There's no use prolonging such an event if they don't respond to compressions and the first couple of doses of medication. Particularly if there's no treatable cause to immediately correct. Further, our group had also been following him. His clinical course had deteriorated steadily, despite any of our interventions. We had repeatedly advised the family as much, but they were having a difficult time accepting the inevitable."

Kristine's brow knitted for only a fraction of a second. She schooled her expression and said, "Did she tell you those things?"

"Yes, and I took a look at the record when I arrived this morning. It was still at the nurses' station. There was no reason for the nurses involved to criticize her decision-making, from what I could see."

"Well, there is more to the situation than I believe you're aware of." She tented her fingers before saying more, then deliberately rested her hands on the desktop. There would be no gesturing, nor flinging around of hands. No show of emotion.

"You see, when Dr. Lange came on board, Dr. Griswold oriented her to the concept of long-term acute care. Including the always-present issue of withdrawal of care in our patients. She expressed understanding, the same understanding she expressed to your pulmonary colleague, who also participated in her on-boarding. She had the opportunity to ask questions of both of them, air her position on advanced directives, and work within the policy or decline the offered position. She accepted and chose to stay." Kristine paused for a second, then apparently thought more information was warranted. "Then, it became known she was pressuring every patient she attended to sign a DNR – do not resuscitate – form."

Formal lecture concluded. *Yes, I know what DNR means.* "How did that become known?"

"I'm not sure what you're asking. Through staff observations, I believe. It became common knowledge she was approaching all her patients, and those she covered on the weekends, to sign or revise their decisions."

Obviously, he wasn't going to get her to confess to running a spy ring, so he let it drop, for the time being. "And would you explain for my benefit again, the exact nature of the policy regarding withdrawal of care? You see, no one in my group has complained about any such policy."

"Yes, well, DNR status is obtained by the nursing staff when the patient is admitted, whether they have a prior signed document or not. That is then posted on the chart. Of course, any patient is free to change their mind during the course of treatment here, and that change will be updated on the chart, as well."

"So, I understand that, of course, but what is this rule about the case manager or Director of Nursing having to agree with the DNR, or the decision to withdraw care. Or being present during such discussions?"

Kristine shifted in her seat, and paused before responding. "That is not exactly true, as you state it. The DON and case manager are to be informed of such decisions or changes in status, but there's no *rule*...it doesn't state they control the decision, or have to be present during those discussions."

"I see. Well, that's good to clear up, because I was concerned that they had assumed a controlling role, perhaps even prohibiting doctors from independent decision-making."

He noted her gaze remained impassive. But the corners of Kristine's mouth twitched as she prepared for her next remark. "At least, that is not my reading of the policy. But I will pull it up and review the wording."

I bet you will. "I'd like a copy of that policy, too, if you don't mind, as it affects our intensivist group."

She glanced at her impressive watch once again. "Certainly. I can do that. If you give me your email, I'll forward it to you this afternoon." She swung around in her chair, signaling that the meeting neared conclusion, and said, "One more issue we haven't touched on, Dr. Meyers, is hope. Here at Oakwood Specialty we feel that all patients and families deserve hope that they or their loved one will survive and regain health so they may be discharged, to home or rehab or whatever venue is the next step for them. Depriving them of hope is a negative, I'm sure you agree, and may impact their chance of survival. You understand that. And your colleagues, among others, also convey hope for recovery to these people during their often-stormy hospital course and intensive care stay. And I would expect that it is not false hope which you impart prior to their transfer here."

End lecture number two.

Why did he feel he'd just been reprimanded or warned, his responsibility for what had happened to an errant pal impressed upon him? With a small smile, Ash produced his business card and slid it across the desk toward her. She picked it up, briefly examined it, and stood. Now, they were really done.

"I'll look forward to receiving your email and the attached policy later today."

She returned his smile and moved toward her office door, swinging it open so he might pass easily.

"You're welcome. I trust our discussion provided a clearer picture." A fairly generic statement coming from an administrator whose secretary sat, all ears, not eight feet away in an open area.

"I appreciate your time," Ash said, turning on his heel and heading straight for the open staircase which descended to the atrium lobby below.

As he reached the ground floor, his cell vibrated in his coat pocket. He stopped, swiped it, and noted his wife's smiling face. She informed him she'd just arrived in Tulsa, ready to hit the ground running.

By comparison, he wasn't so sure he had accomplished much of anything.

SEVEN

The afternoon waning, Ash sat at his desk, his office door closed. He'd finished seeing his scheduled renal patients and wanted to make this phone call before he left. It was wise to ask Griswold directly what his take was on Dr. Lange and what was portrayed as her anti-resuscitation campaign. Ash had the facility's policy before him, and had read it twice, digesting the legalese before calling the head of the internal medicine group. At least Kristine Nelson had followed through.

The cell rang three times, before the internist picked up. "Griswold here."

"Hey, Todd, Ash Meyers."

"Ash, how're you?"

"Good, good. Say, do you have a minute?"

"Sure. Give me a second. Let me close down this chart." Ash heard a clunking sound, then movement, then Griswold came back on the line. Sounded as if he was walking to a better location for a talk. "Okay, what's up?" he asked. "I just saw the lady in two-o-four, Smith. Seems she's improving with your dialysis." Ash heard a door close.

"Yeah. We're pleased with her improvement. Probably

30

continue it for another week or so. See how she does. If she doesn't develop any more problems, she should make steady progress after that."

"Good."

"But I'm calling about something else. There was an issue which came to my attention last week." As the words left his mouth, Ash realized the internist probably feared he was calling about that climbing creatinine he'd missed over the previous weekend. But, hey, a little fear was not such a bad thing.

Todd Griswold cleared his throat. "Yeah?"

"It surprised me to hear that Erica Lange was fired this past weekend. And I wondered what caused that?"

The other doctor didn't answer right away. Moments later, he said, "A couple of things. But, I don't see that it should concern you."

The internist's comment and tone irritated him. Ash said, "Usually it wouldn't. But I walked in on her and Raina last Friday in the doctors' office, and she was pretty upset. What she told me sounded odd, about a code last Thursday. I just thought I'd get more information from you."

Griswold said nothing, so Ash continued, "I also spoke with Kristine Nelson earlier today, and she sent me the policy on withdrawal of care. I'd heard that doctors had to check with the case manager or Director of Nursing before making a patient DNR. Or there was a question about that. Some sort of rule or something. The policy doesn't use that kind of language."

"Question in whose mind?"

"Well, Erica's for one. And now mine."

"To be frank, Erica has issues."

"Okay, fair enough. But she mentioned she felt like the nurses were keeping track – like spying on her – reporting to Ric Newman whenever she discussed resuscitation with patients or families."

"Spying? That's absurd." His tone even more irritable, he went on, "Look, I've counseled her several times about

31

this. It seems she's convinced all these patients have reached the end of the road, and don't deserve to be resuscitated. She acts like she's on a mission or something. We finally just had to let her go. It's all documented in her file, and I'm not going to reverse my decision if that's what you're asking me to do."

"Not asking that, Todd. Just trying to ascertain the facts. If such a rule exists or is practiced, that affects our intensivist group, too. And if case managers or the Director of Nursing are involving themselves in complicated medical decision-making, then the whole of the policy requires further discussion with all the staff doctors and administration. And probably the lawyers."

Griswold assumed a conciliatory tone. "Look, she was pressuring patients to declare themselves DNR, which I don't believe is justified in all cases. We have a different philosophy of care here, that's all. She just didn't seem to understand the concept of long-term acute care, and frankly didn't belong in this practice setting. In my opinion."

"Okay, I get what you're saying. Sounds like it was a problem for more than a few weeks."

"That's right. And that's just paranoid to think the nurses were spying on her, or any of the doctors."

"I understand your point. Well, I'll let you go. I wanted to get your perspective on the situation, and I appreciate your comments." Ash paused, then said, "Because I would be concerned if there were standing policies, or policies in development for that matter, which restricted honest discussions with patients. Or if our autonomous function as physicians was curtailed or infringed upon. I'm sure you understand."

Griswold said nothing.

Ash finished with, "Thanks, Todd. I'll be back on next week. If you think of anything else, just let me know."

"Right," Griswold replied. They disconnected.

Ash sat at his desk for a moment, gathering his thoughts. He had to make one more call that evening to settle this thing, and he dreaded the whole prospect. What a jumbled mess of conflicting impressions. Kristine Nelson and Todd Griswold were at least rather defensive, and at most weren't leveling with him. Something didn't fit. But maybe he was reading too much into the whole scenario. He hadn't really accomplished much meeting with or calling those two, had he? Other than playing the unwelcome role of protector or avenger. And it didn't quite ring true that Erica was paranoid, not from what he'd seen of her. But who knew?

He shut down his computer, shoved the written policy in his small flat case, and headed out of his private office. June was gone; quiet had descended.

It was time to go home, let the dog out, and prepare for an interesting evening, alone.

~ ~ ~ ~

Relaxing in his study, with Roberta lounging at his feet, Ash glanced at a picture of Margo and him on a recent vacation. Just the two of them. He was anxious to hear how her day had gone, and he needed to get this call out of the way so he could move on. Having waited until Erica's dinner was likely done, and her kids settled, he dialed the now familiar number.

She picked up after just two rings. "Hello?"

Surprised that she sounded as if she was uncertain of the caller, he assumed a more formal tone. "This is Ash Meyers calling." He certainly didn't want to say Dr. Meyers. They had already passed that milestone in their professional relationship, at least over the past few days.

"Hi, Ash. How're you?"

"Fine. Good. I said I would get back to you on this issue at Specialty."

"Right," she affirmed.

He noted her expectant tone. This wasn't going to be easy. "I spoke with Kristine Nelson today. We had a good discussion, I believe, about your situation there, and she forwarded me the policy regarding withdrawal of care."

"Good."

"I was a little unsure during our conversation whether she was saying this was a hard and fast rule that they have about clearing patient's wishes with the case manager or Director of Nursing, or whether doctors can exercise independent judgement with patients and families about the matter. So, seeing the policy helped. Somewhat."

"What do you mean, exactly?"

"It's not a strict rule, but the language leaves some latitude about how the staff may approach the decision. I mentioned to her and Griswold that it was troublesome if the staff could override doctors' medical decision-making."

"Wait, you talked with Todd Griswold, too?"

"Yes, I did."

On the tail of a heavy sigh, she said, "Well, that's not going to help me."

"I'm afraid you may be right."

"What did he say?"

"He seemed fairly defensive, and wondered, of course, why I had any interest in this. He went on to say that you all had discussed the philosophy of the long-term acute care model on more than one occasion. And that Kristine Nelson had also met with you, as did one of my partners. It seems they think this is not a new position you've taken."

She conveyed a sharper tone when she next said, "Well, there are some other factors I've uncovered which you may not be aware of." She paused for effect.

"Such as?"

"Well, for one thing, Raina Crawford found out – and I don't know how – that the nursing staff is incentivized to push for full codes on everyone."

"What do you mean?"

"Yes, well, apparently they receive stipends or payments for their required continuing nursing education each year if they keep people alive. Even racking up points toward tuition for higher nursing degrees."

"That's quite a charge. Are you sure of that?"

"You bet it is. And there's sort of a competition between them."

Ash couldn't believe what he was hearing. Was Griswold right? Was Erica fundamentally off her rocker? Or had this colleague scratched the surface of a deeper, more sinister problem?

"And there's more."

He didn't cut in.

"Raina says she's overheard nurses comparing notes on their shift scheduling. A few disgruntled nurses complain that they get more night shifts, weekends, and holidays than the others, because they don't think it's right, either, to code everyone. In other words, paying some nurses *in kind* for their cooperation or efforts."

She didn't have to explain. He got it. And his recently eaten dinner churned.

She continued. "And better performance reviews, promise of unit manager positions, stuff like that. Ash, this may be an issue of maintaining heads in the beds." She stopped there and let it lay.

Ash got her point immediately. "Okay, look, if what you say is true, that's a very serious charge...against the facility."

The specter of insurance and Medicare fraud pushed into his thoughts, looming large. What had he gotten himself involved in here? He needed to deliver his final verdict on her future at Oakwood, which was basically nil, and conclude this conversation. Then, he'd consider whether any further interventions on this other front were necessary.

"Bottom line, Erica, I need to be honest and tell you that Griswold, as well as Kristine Nelson, will not reverse their decision regarding your termination. They've made that clear to me. And there isn't anything else I can do about that."

She remained silent on the other end for several moments. He fought the urge to just hang up, and pretend they'd been disconnected when she next spoke.

"I'm really sorry to hear that. I thought, with the position your group enjoys there, that you could make them see to reason. I felt they made a knee-jerk decision and that you speaking up would make them reconsider."

"I got the impression it wasn't just a one-off situation, Erica."

"Look, I'm sorry to involve you in this. It's obvious you feel you're not in a position to help…"

Re-orienting her then, he said, "I've done what we agreed I would do. Met with Nelson, and I spoke with Griswold. At this point my role is not key. It's probably best, Erica, if you call it a day and move on. There, no doubt, are other positions more to your liking which you can pursue."

"I don't know about that, since I'm not legally supposed to take my kids and haul off to some other part of the country."

A career and divorce counselor he had no desire to become. He reiterated, "I think it's best if you let it go."

"You may be right, but we'll see." She abruptly hung up.

Yes, they would see. But, he didn't desire his future to become entangled with hers. He could now check that off his list. Done.

Hearing no further voices, Roberta stirred and got to her feet. It was time to run the dog outside. And telephone Margo.

EIGHT

Wednesday

She knew what she'd heard last week. Before the code blue, that awful turning point. His wife was a decorator of some local renown, and was to be out of town this week. Was it Tulsa? Something like that. Opportunity to pursue this issue was not exhausted, not to her mind, anyway, no matter what he'd said or implied last night.

Erica sat in her home office, turning her focus to new emails, and checking her old residency colleagues on Facebook. They all sounded so solid in their subspecialty choices, smug in their careers. She often wished she'd gone for further fellowship training after her medicine residency. Might have avoided all this frustration with practice, or at least she might have been more satisfied with her opportunities. But at thirty-nine, it was too late now to change course that drastically. Especially by herself with two kids on board. No, she'd have to find something else.

She glanced at the wall clock. It was 1:30 P.M. Her son and daughter, age eight and ten, would be out of school in a couple of hours. Today they would ride the bus home. She could get them organized and fed, then drop them at her

37

sister's, who was an angel and never minded having them visit their only cousin for a few hours. A temporarily-retired teacher, she had even confessed she liked helping kids with their homework. How perfect! And tonight Erica would throw in their pajamas for good measure, so they'd be ready to drop into bed when they returned home, hopefully not too late for a school night. So, a wonderful solution to her evening plans came into sharp focus.

~ ~ ~ ~

"Mommy," her eight-year-old Reynolds whined, "why do we have to go to Aunt Susie's again? I want to stay home."

"I have to do some extra work this evening, hon. It won't take that long, and you'll be home before you know it."

His sister reminded her younger brother, "It's the medical call thing, stupid."

"Riley, don't talk to your brother like that. You both have homework, and Auntie Sue can help you with that. Samantha will be busy with hers, too. And you can grab a quick bath and get into your pj's. Before you know it, I'll pick you up."

"I'm caught up," Riley announced, "but I have my big project for next week. And I don't want *him* bothering me." She made a face at her brother, who returned the expression which Erica caught in the rearview mirror. She chose to ignore that one and drove on.

"Okay, look, we're almost there."

Erica took a right at the next corner, drove about half a block, and turned into her sister's driveway. At last, she could proceed unencumbered.

~ ~ ~ ~

The doorbell rang twice before it registered with Ash. Rather odd, that time of the evening. He wasn't expecting anyone to come calling. He checked his cell phone for the camera image, shocked at what, or who, he saw. There she stood on his covered porch, glancing this way and that. Perhaps he should just ignore her.

His curiosity overcame his gut-level feeling, as he made his way through the kitchen, front hall to the foyer, then paused before opening the door. Roberta let out one unconvincing bark.

"Sit, girl." Which she did, and commenced brushing the floor with her wagging tail.

In the soft light of the paired porch lanterns Erica Lange stood there in tight jeans, a sporty knee-length coat, tall boots, and a soft cowl neck sweater. She bore a slouchy leather bag slung over her right shoulder to complete her look. He surmised she hadn't just sat around the house all day garbed as she appeared then. All he knew was that she looked fabulous and was on his front porch, apparently seeking admittance.

"Hello, there," he said, attempting to fill the frame of his wide entry door.

She smiled, spread her hands outward, and replied, "Hi."

"This is a surprise." How awkward it was fast becoming to maintain a colleague on his front porch, and not offer some sort of invitation to enter.

"I hope not too much of one."

He gave up, took a step backwards, saying, "Why don't you come in?"

Roberta rose, smiling and wagging, apparently deciding this was to be a friendly visit. Their old standard poodle Gloria – God rest her soul – would not have been the welcoming party Roberta was.

Without speaking, Erica entered the house. As she stepped past him, he couldn't help but detect the subtle fragrance she wore. What was this woman up to?

They stood and regarded each other for a moment until Ash regained his manners, offered to take her coat, and suggested they move to the kitchen. He'd been busy in there anyway, and he didn't want to lounge about in the great room, socializing. Margo might call any minute. They made their way down the long hall, Ash leading the way, with Roberta covering their rear flank.

Arriving in the kitchen, he asked, "May I get you something to drink?" hoping she wouldn't request a whiskey. There was going to be no imbibing.

She glanced around, then said, "Oh, just some water."

He produced a glass from a nearby cabinet, and while turning to the refrigerator dispenser, asked, "So what brings you by this evening?"

"Well, I didn't like the way we left it last night."

He turned around, stared at her, and finally recovered enough to serve her the ice water, placing it on the counter where she'd taken a seat. Roberta had settled herself across the room but lay oriented toward them, ever observant. Ash remained standing near the sink, the kitchen counter a solid barrier between them.

"Oh?"

"Yes. I felt bad after I essentially hung up on you. I do appreciate all you've done to help with this situation. I wanted you to know that." She sipped water and threw him a little shoulder.

"All right. But you could have just sent me an email or text."

"You're right, of course." She smiled. "But you made a special effort most wouldn't on behalf of a colleague, and I wanted to thank you in person."

"You're welcome."

"Now that you've had some time to think about what I told you last night, I'm wondering what thoughts you might have about the larger issues."

He wasn't going to admit to her, right then and there, that the issues she'd broached had bothered him all day. Kept popping to mind when he'd had a moment between patients. But he'd refrained from running to his managing partner to discuss the observations and reports she'd relayed, and the impact it might have on their group. At least up to that point he had refrained. How to verify what Erica had said was the next step, if he chose to take a next step at all.

"I thought what you said about the incentives was very troublesome, even outrageous. But those charges need to be verified. And I'm not saying Raina Crawford is dishonest, but it's serious enough to warrant vetting. Don't you think?"

"I agree, but I believe her. We've both observed the nurses' behavior, and it's consistent with something like that going on. But, I'm sure we can drum up some more evidence, if that's what you want."

"Look, Erica, I don't personally *want* to open some investigation into Oakwood and its staff. Our group goes there as consultants, and we've enjoyed a good relationship for some time with the organization. I would need a lot more solid evidence of questionable activity going on before I'd go to my group and discuss it, or hammer on the administration or Griswold."

She'd assumed a pouty, downcast expression as he spoke, then suddenly looked up and smiled. "Okay, I can agree with that. So, will you consider staying in touch, especially if I can produce more facts, more evidence?"

Roberta rose and stood by the back door, her tail in motion. She caught Ash's eye.

"Perhaps. I might consider that. Excuse me, I need to let her out."

"Won't she run off?" Erica swiveled and regarded his dog. "Do we need to go outside?"

"No, there's an invisible fence. She won't run off."

Erica slid off the barstool as Ash completed his task and returned to the counter. "Well, I should be off. Thanks for inviting me in, and at least discussing this with me once more."

"It's okay, but let me know if you wish to speak again, before coming over."

"Is your wife here? I'd like to meet her...I've heard so much about her design business recently." She glanced

41

around the large kitchen area, acting as if Margo might materialize at any moment.

His guard up, Ash said, "No, she's in Tulsa on a big commercial project."

"Oh, sounds like she's a busy woman."

Ash regarded Erica before answering. "That she is. I'll see you to the front door now. I'm sure *you* must be busy with your kids this evening."

Bam...throw her children back at her. Where had she stashed them, anyway? Or did she leave them alone when she had to take call or go back in? He picked up her coat, handed it to her, and headed through the main hall toward their foyer. Time for this lady to leave.

Having reached the door first, hand on the knob, he turned slightly only to find Erica crowding his space. She wore a look he'd seen often enough. Her black eyes flashed. Before he could react, she placed a warm hand on his chest, and standing on her tiptoes, planted a kiss on his right cheek, somewhat more than a little peck. Her perfume filled his nostrils.

Very nearly overcome, he slowly removed her hand from his torso, and said, "Dr. Lange," before he failed to stop himself. Moving backward then, he opened the door wide so as to give her ample room to exit. She smiled, slipped on her coat, and moved through the offered opening.

"Goodnight," she said brightly before she stepped off the brick porch.

Ash stood stunned, door wide open, as Roberta bounded around the corner of the garage and parking court. She barked once at Erica, saying her goodbyes to the departing woman.

"Hey, there Robie, goodbye to you, too."

Now, this was too much...presuming to nickname his dog.

A thought then intruded...*thank goodness dogs can't talk.*

~ ~ ~ ~

Erica watched from her car as Ash welcomed the friendly Golden inside and shut the front door. Through the massive dining room windows, she watched him navigate the corridor toward the kitchen.

She pulled away, waited just beyond his driveway for five minutes while he killed several lights in the main portion of the house. Had he retired for the night, or was he in his study calling his wife? She'd noticed that wonderful room, a true library, off the foyer when she had entered. Nothing shabby about that place.

It was time to finish this visit. She messed her hair, smeared her lipstick, and removed one of her large loop earrings.

Pulling away from the curb, she made a quick U-turn then stopped in front of Ash's long drive, just a portion of his large home visible in the background through the residential forest. She quickly got out of her car, cell phone in hand, and stood with her back to the house, snapping a few selfies. No smiles permitted. She then commenced a brief selfie video recording, describing how he'd called her to come over, with his wife out of town no less, wanting to discuss their unfinished conversation of the previous night. How she'd been so naïve about his obvious intentions. How he'd offered her something to drink, how he'd grabbed her as she tried to leave. Pure and simple sexual harassment, maybe even assault. And she'd never expected it of him. Such a shame.

She stopped the recording, pocketed her phone, and slipped into her car. Straightening her appearance, she smiled. It was past time to pick up the kids.

NINE

Thursday

The call came in right in the middle of a new patient visit. At first, Dr. Meyers ignored the vibrating device in his pocket, as it was not his custom to take calls during patient appointments.

He'd get to it when he had a break. Likely, it wasn't Margo or one of the kids calling him that time of the morning.

Cranky didn't adequately describe his mood that morning. Disgusted was more like it. And he was working hard to conceal his attitude and fatigue from the patients and staff. June had already picked up on it, and was treading lightly or keeping her distance altogether.

To say he'd slept fitfully was also an understatement. He'd fallen asleep later than usual after a brief call from Margo. Her weariness had diverted attention from his obvious up-tight tone, leading her to believe they both just needed a good night's sleep. At least he hoped that was her conclusion.

He spent the following hours tossing and turning, the victim of weird dream fragments intruding at will. Finally

44

rising around five thirty, he gave up on the night, hoping the light of day would smooth his thoughts. It was no good keeping situations like this from his wife. But he had hoped he could control it, bring it to a swift conclusion, deliver a summary report to her, and move on. But now, he wasn't so sure that was the course unfolding before him.

His cell beeped with a voicemail notice. Erica. God almighty, was this woman never going to give up? He stopped listening immediately, hit save, and returned his attention to the medical record before him, and his dictation. Obviously, he needed to exert a firm hand, ignore his usual diplomacy employed during professional encounters, and get this straightened out. No more mister nice guy routine.

~ ~ ~ ~

Ric Newman stood in the door of the room, aghast at the scene unfolding. He felt a presence at his left elbow, and glanced at Kristine Nelson who had joined the small crowd. He signaled her with a shake of the head, insuring her restraint, at least for the next several minutes.

The ninety-two-year-old woman lay on the bed, her gown askew, while a nurse rhythmically compressed her tiny chest. On cue, respiratory therapy delivered a breath through the Ambu bag. Two nurses prepared various resuscitation medications, including a third dose of epinephrine. This had been going on for fifteen minutes, and no apparent change in the woman's status had resulted.

Ric turned aside.

Kristine followed him into the hall just outside the patient's door. "You look upset," she observed.

Ric grimaced. "She wasn't supposed to be coded. The family made that clear from the get-go. And produced her signed document." He glanced back in the room. "I hope we haven't broken every rib in her poor little body."

That elicited a frown from Kristine. She surveyed the room again. Just as she turned back to Ric, two women

45

marched toward the patient's room, distress written all over their faces.

"What the hell is going on in there?" the older one asked, while her younger sister pushed aside anyone partially obstructing the door, shouldering her way into the room. Both of them arriving at their mother's bedside, the eldest made clear their position to the entire west wing of the facility.

"Stop...stop this right now!"

"What are you doing?" screamed her younger sister. "We have papers...she has papers!"

The nurse delivering compressions paused for a moment and threw the attending doctor a look, while respiratory therapy delivered one more ventilation then paused as well. Dr. Griswold held up a hand, then indicated they should resume as he turned aside to the distraught family.

"You are her daughters?"

"Yes, yes," the older daughter yelled. "Stop this!"

"Are you her DPOA?"

"Yes, and this is against her wishes. Go get the papers!"

Ric caught Griswold's eye and, turning on his heel, headed to the nurses' station in search of the woman's paperwork. *We had better get this under control right now.*

When he hurriedly returned to the room, he could tell before stepping inside that the code had been called. Quiet, save for the sisters' sobbing, filled the space. They both sat on their mother's bed, holding her hand, stroking her face and hair, the bed covers now pulled up to her neck.

Near the door, Kristine Nelson stared. Todd Griswold walked away from the scene, his face impassive. He gave her a sharp nod as he passed by. She didn't budge, apparently cemented in place at the sight.

Ric turned away, leaving Kristine in the doorway, and retreated to his office to regroup alone. He hoped she didn't follow. What a miserable situation. In due time that day, he would review what happened with the nurses involved. This mistake was intolerable.

46

~ ~ ~ ~

An impatient Kristine Nelson gazed out her office windows, waiting on hold. Never had she seen such a scene. It wasn't her habit to attend codes, feeling she had no role in such clinical situations. And she wished she'd not ventured a peek at that one.

An MBA by education, she had never studied nursing or medicine, pharmacy, nor anything else medical along the way, other than health administration in graduate school. That had not equipped her for what really went on in the trenches. What a ghastly routine...pounding on someone's chest, sticking tubes down their throats, shocking them and watching their body jerk. How totally awful! You'd think by this point in the twenty-first century some other more graceful method of bringing people back from the grave's edge would have been devised. Apparently not.

"Well, hello, Kristine Nelson," came the smooth male voice, interrupting her thoughts.

"Hello, Chase."

"I trust you're doing well."

"Well enough," Kristine answered stiffly.

"How may I assist you on this fine fall day?"

The forty-five-year-old VP's tone irritated her on the heels of that horrible scene. She refused to abide his patronizing manner any longer. "I need some of your time to discuss a situation which has developed here, and worsened over the past several weeks."

"Something to do with strategic planning?"

"You might say."

She heard muffled sounds as he apparently sought his office chair and fiddled with his computer. "Do you expect this to be a long discussion?"

Kristine took her seat as well, and pulled up his professionally retouched smiling face on the corporation's website. She wanted to look at him as she spoke. "It could be."

47

"Well, I have more time this afternoon. Have to be in another meeting in ten minutes, but why don't you give me the gist of the situation? Then we can discuss further later today."

"Very well. The chief of our internal medicine group here fired one of the staff internists last weekend over the issue of withdrawal of care. It may have repercussions for the facility and, I hazard to say, the entire company."

"How so?"

"She maintains that we do not respect patient's wishes regarding end-of-life procedures. She's solicited the help of another subspecialist doctor, who discussed this issue with me on her behalf earlier this week. He seemed to be on a fact-finding mission. Honestly, we've always felt she had some sort of agenda to make all the patients here DNR."

"Who's we?"

"The head of the internal medicine group, the director of nursing, and myself."

"Well, this sounds like a discussion which does require more time. Are you worried about how she was terminated?"

"To some degree, though we crossed all our 'T's', dotted our 'I's' in the process. But I do see some vulnerability for the organization."

"Vulnerability?"

"Right. I believe so."

"Okay. Listen, I've got to run. Why don't we schedule another call for later, say around four thirty this afternoon? Will that work for you?"

"I'll make it work. Talk with you then."

Kristine hung up, and rose from her chair. Frustrated and worried, she stood at her windows and opened the blinds wider. The numerous large oaks – strong and sturdy – decorating the hospital's lawn sported fall's hues, some yellow, others shades of rust. Usually a lovely sight to enjoy for weeks. But that day, a low grey ceiling hung over the city, well-defined dark clouds pressing downward. Her mood now matched the forecast – a cold front approaching, good chance of severe storms, then clearing by the weekend. Or, in her case, likely some time later.

Could she get herself through all that and land on the other side unscathed? Uncertainty nagged. She'd had about enough of Chase Monroe, but did she dare confront him, press him? With what he knew? Perhaps another discussion the first of next week with the white knight Dr. Meyers was in order. But should she wait that long? Mustering her resolve, she turned away from the windows. She'd have to.

After this anticipated discussion with Monroe was history.

~ ~ ~ ~

His hand barely touched the car door handle when he heard a voice behind him. Swiveling around and still gripping the handle, Ash watched her emerge from behind a cement column in the parking garage. *What?* He straightened to his full height.

"What are you doing here?"

"Waiting for you." Erica replied.

"That's obvious. Look, Erica, this is not good. You can't keep popping up or hanging around. If you and I need to discuss anything more, it has to be scheduled and in an appropriate place."

"Well, I can't meet you at the hospital, or your office, right? So, I'm getting creative."

"Creative isn't the word I'd use. I need to get home...what do *you* need?"

"Your time and interest. Look, I know this seems weird, and I apologize for last night. I just reacted to your kindness without thinking. I shouldn't have, and I'm ashamed." She lowered her eyes. A moment later, she locked eyes again and asked, "Can you get past that, and just listen one more time?"

Unnecessary harshness wasn't going to work here. "All right. We can talk one more time, but not now."

She brightened. "Thank you. How about we get coffee

49

later tomorrow, say around five. Will you be done with office by then?"

"Probably. Where?"

"How about Chisholm's, the grill over on 119th?"

"Okay. I'll agree now to meet you there, but I'll text ahead of time if I'm running behind and can't make it. Tomorrow's busy."

"I understand, Ash. Thanks." She backed away and turned toward the garage stairwell, obviously not parked on that level.

How had she found his car anyway? Of course…it was sitting on the drive the other night where she could plainly see what he drove and his license plate. So, had she spent her afternoon walking all these levels just scouting it out? This woman had some nerve. He watched her retreat, then eased himself into his vehicle, checked his rearview mirror, backed out and slowly drove away. He'd plan for this next meeting very thoroughly, control the whole scene, and end these encounters once and for all. Right?

TEN

Friday

He stepped through the heavy door and spotted her right off the bat. How could he not? Her dark hair stood out among that of other patrons. He could see, even from a distance, that she hadn't spared a hand with her preparations that evening. But with her deep, dark eyes, thick lashes, and sharp brows, she hardly required much enhancing. Perish those thoughts, he reminded himself. He'd come prepared to control the discussion, and her. Focusing on her beauty would create an impediment to that goal, for sure. He wove his way through the tables.

A full wine glass sat before her. "Care to sit?" she asked with a smile.

He slid into the small booth across from her without a word.

"So, you got away despite a busy day. I'm glad it worked out." She took a sip.

Ash glanced around and caught their waitress' eye. Motioning her over, he requested coffee, black, and redirected his gaze to Erica. He finally spoke.

"Yeah, it was busy. So, tell me, what is the need to

51

continue our previous discussion? Nothing has changed since Sunday evening, nor Tuesday or Wednesday night for that matter."

"Oh, I beg to differ. I think you'll be interested in what I have to say."

Their waitress arrived with his steaming coffee, suspending conversation for a few moments. He thanked her and when she retreated, he picked up again.

"Oh?"

"Yes." Her black eyes flashed. "It seems I have options."

"Good. I'm glad you've found another position."

"Well, not exactly, yet. And I don't know if you'd call it a position, in the usual sense of the word."

Oh boy, what was she talking about? He could imagine red flags sprouting all over the tabletop, and he'd better pay attention. He doubted she'd arranged to meet so she could inform him of a new job opportunity, or that her ex gave her permission to leave the state and take the kids.

"So, what kind of position are you referring to?"

"The position I'm in."

Now he was really skeptical. This was not a new job she referred to. "Okay, Erica, be more specific. What are you getting at?"

She leaned in over the table, mashing her breasts on the tabletop. He didn't miss her show of cleavage. In a mysterious tone she said, "My position of wrongful termination." After her pronouncement, she straightened, leaned back, and threw him a challenging look.

He settled back against the cushy booth, putting distance between them. He was not going to whisper with this woman across some table in a bar and grill. Wary, he glanced around, and though it was busier, saw no one he recognized in the immediate area. His gaze swung back to Erica.

"How do you figure?"

"Well, I checked the labor laws. Even though the state is an employment-at-will state, the group has a contract with Oakwood, and I had a contract with the group. There's language about *cause* and *without cause*, but it's rather vague. They can't just dump me or anyone else willy-nilly. Which they could if no contract existed. And there are merit laws here which govern how terminations under these contracts are handled."

Examining labor laws had never quite captured his interest, and he wasn't going to debate with her over any particulars. She seemed to have studied up. Maybe she should explore going to law school.

"Interesting, but don't you think that's a stretch? In their minds, they may believe they had cause and have documented such. Lawyers construct all those contracts. They're pretty standard, and cover the bases. Plus, Griswold, or Kristine Nelson, likely took sufficient care to avoid you being able to bring such a case."

She threw her head from side to side, acting as if she'd anticipated his objections.

"Precisely. I believe they were keeping an eye on me, through the nurses, and falsely documenting my care of patients. Even my discussions with patients. Building a case."

"Why, Erica, would they single you out for scrutiny?" He pushed his cooling coffee aside.

"Because, as I've said, they didn't like the fact that I counseled patients and families about care withdrawal and DNR's."

Time for a big dose of reality. "Look, I'm not sure that was what you thought it was. Nurses are always observing our interactions with patients and families. And they don't always agree with what we say or do. But leveling a spying charge at them is a bit much."

"Well, if it happened to you, I bet you'd see it differently."

"Okay, but going after them is a long, hard course to pursue. I'd think about that more than once before taking that tack. Have you consulted an attorney, maybe someone who does labor law?"

She ignored his question, and said, "And I may sue the

upper-level executives at the corporate offices, and the corporation as a whole."

"What?"

"You doing okay?" Ash looked up at the voice. Their waitress had been replaced by an energetic young waiter who was making the rounds. He clarified, "Need anything here?"

"Yes. I'll have a beer," Ash said abruptly, momentarily forgetting the place housed a microbrewery and offered dozens of selections.

The waiter smiled, "Which one?" He handed Ash a skinny laminated list, both sides full of choices.

"Oh, right…just the Boulevard Wheat," he said, pointing to the first thing which caught his eye.

"A good choice, and for you, ma'am?"

"I'll have another of this pinot…the Beaux Frere."

"Excellent." And off he went to fulfill his mission.

Ash focused on Erica again. He braced his elbows and leaned forward. "That is a big deal, Doctor. You'll have to gather a lot of damning information to make it out of the starting blocks."

"I asked you the other night if you would help me if I found more evidence, real evidence. Which I have."

"Wait a minute. I don't recall agreeing to help you if more evidence appears. I believe you asked if I would *consider* staying in touch if you found more evidence, and I said, 'Perhaps I would *consider* that.' I didn't promise to investigate with you or for you."

"All right." She threw him a warm smile. "You know, you *are* so smart. And such a mind for details. I should have expected you'd remember our conversation. Very clearly."

The pit in his stomach complained just as their waiter appeared with their new drinks. He took a quick sip of the beer, and said, "I think I'll order something to eat. You?"

"Sure," Erica agreed.

The enthusiastic waiter seemed more than pleased. Their orders placed, he hustled away. Ash swigged more beer.

"So, aren't you going to wait and eat with your wife?"

she asked. "I'm sorry to keep you so close to dinner."

"She's still out of town."

Oops. And hadn't called him the previous evening. As soon as the words left his mouth, he realized his tone sounded a bit sour. He better watch it, he reminded himself, that he not convey, especially to this woman seated across from him, any hint of disenchantment with his lovely wife.

"I see." Erica sipped her wine, and eyed Ash. "So, you don't think I should pursue the facility, or any of the individuals involved with my termination?"

"Not at this point, no. But, as I've already said, I suggest you consult a lawyer before you make a final decision...or any rash moves. It could go very badly, Erica."

"I suppose so." She assumed a thoughtful expression while sipping wine, then said, "Things are not as they appear there. Bigger things than even I believed at first."

"You mentioned some of that Tuesday evening when I called back."

"Yes. This scheme to keep people alive as long as possible, even with the inevitable facing them, is just not right. I do believe they are promoting a heads-in-the-beds initiative for billing purposes. That's corruption, and it could represent Medicare and insurance fraud. And the incentives offered to nurses to help them with that...it all stinks to high heaven."

Their waiter returned with their plates.

Having drained his first glass, Ash ordered another beer. All that done, and the waiter gone, he responded to her last comment. "I recall you mentioned that. How sure are you? How do you know all this?"

"Oh, I've got my sources." She looked smug as she pushed food around on her small plate.

He swigged beer and dove into his meal. "Sources, plural?"

"I'll not say."

Oh man, she was either in possession of some real information, or was making this whole thing up.

55

Embellishment, at least, seemed to be one of her strong suits.

"You're making serious accusations, Erica, and you'll need to substantiate them if you're going to pursue this. I don't want to know who's feeding you information, but I'd say it better be someone reliable, and good. And you need to cover your ass." Oops, again...the buzz had hit him, and that just somehow slipped out.

She smiled. "I like your firm tone."

And he liked her saying so. She was really quite beautiful, so vulnerable, in fact, and his rapid consumption of beer was helping him gain an enhanced appreciation for her plight. This woman needed someone to assist her, guide her through this process, and make sure she didn't do something stupid. She had two little kids, after all. He might just be the right person, but he'd be careful, of course.

He smiled. "That's what it takes in situations like this."

"Absolutely."

In a wise tone, he added, "Again, I'd advise you to consult with an attorney about the labor law issues first, then get their opinion about the other larger situation. And be prepared to deliver real evidence to whomever you consult." He was repeating himself, for sure, but maybe the third time would sink in.

"Oh, you sound so right. And I think that's very good advice."

He smiled, "I can check around and find out who's good in this area."

"Oh, would you? That sounds terrific and I'd appreciate that. Very much."

Finished with his food, he settled back with the remains of his beer.

ELEVEN

The garage door slid down, almost soundlessly. It was later than he'd expected, and he needed to get inside and take Roberta out. The third beer had been a bit much, but he'd made it home okay without getting pulled over.

Encouraged by the inviting atmosphere at the grill, and Erica's obvious appreciation for his input, he had lingered. When he'd inquired about her kids, she'd gladly engaged with him, describing her intelligent, charming children. She displayed pictures on her cell. Admittedly, they were darling, just like their mother. And where were they that night? She informed him they were at her sister's for a sleepover with their delightful cousin. It conjured memories of his own two sons in their earlier years, their dear faces and silly antics, and noisy sleepovers he and Margo had endured. Long gone were those days. In turn, she'd asked to see pictures of them, which he'd proudly displayed. What handsome young men, she'd said.

During their whole extended conversation, he'd more than once wondered about her jerk ex-husband, who'd taken off to another state with a new babe. How could anyone do

57

that to this woman?

Standing on the empty driveway in the full moonlight, he waited on Roberta to finish her business and return to the front lawn. He'd not heard from Margo, but he hadn't called her either, particularly not this late and after too many beers. No doubt, she was busy with the new client. Hopefully, not too busy, though, on that Friday evening. A natural beauty, his wife often garnered male attention, her relaxed manner quickly putting men at ease. Perhaps Mr. Tulsa was interested not only in his bare framed-in building, but now also in his fully-finished designer and her superb ideas. Hopefully not too much.

It took more than a moment for him to realize what was happening when a small red Toyota SUV pulled into the drive. Out stepped Erica, tight jeans and all, wearing a smile.

Roberta bounded up, which he hardly noticed, wagging and bouncing with excitement. *A visitor!*

Erica locked her car and approached.

Ash stood and stared as Roberta jumped on first him, then the surprise visitor. "Down girl," was all he could muster.

"I thought I'd see if you arrived home safely. You had quite a lot of beer in a short time there."

"Yeah, I made it. I'm okay."

Roberta, done with greeting everyone, bounded to the front door and waited patiently for assistance. Ash turned and moved toward the front porch, suddenly at a loss for words. He wasn't used to a woman, or women, just showing up unexpectedly. He thought they'd said all they needed to, and more, before departing the grill.

When he reached the door and opened it, he sensed Erica close behind, but chose to avoid a confrontation in his near space. Roberta ran in and made her way to the mudroom to slurp water. Ash stepped inside and pivoted. There she stood on his porch, an expectant look plastered on her face. God, she was beautiful!

He heard himself say, "Do you want to come in?"

"I do." Several steps into the hall, she turned and smiled. He shut the door slowly, knowing full well this was a mistake. It had been a long time since he'd been in such a position, and it intrigued him as he considered what she might do next. Admittedly, the whole scene – exciting, yes, and also dangerous. But, hey, he could handle whatever. Right?

He turned to face her. "Erica, you shouldn't have come by."

"I know."

"Do you need something?"

"You could say." A mysterious smile crept across her face. "How about a glass of water?"

Disarmed, he released a held breath, and pivoting, led the way to his kitchen. How had he let his colorful imaginings get the better of him? Fool that he was, he'd assumed she was after him. Yes, she's unpredictable, but surely not as dangerous as he'd imagined. He'd get her a glass of water, and one for himself, and calm down.

They reached his expansive kitchen. He prepared two ice waters, and handed hers across the counter. In his peripheral vision, he noted Roberta calmly making her way down the hall toward the master bedroom to take up her post in their oversized closet. She certainly seemed unconcerned, obviously calling it a night. He needed to as well.

"Here, why don't we sit down for a few minutes?" he suggested, taking a bar stool near where she stood. "Is there anything more we need to discuss?" He'd not intended to ask such a question, but saying something seemed in order.

After arranging herself on an adjacent stool, she said, "I don't know, maybe. We've covered a lot this evening, but I want you to know again how much I appreciate all you're doing." She leaned in a bit and smiled. "I don't know too many people who would go the extra mile as you've done. Who'd care enough to do that? Empathy is, I guess, what you'd call it."

He stared at her enchanting eyes. God, she'd read him

like a book. Yes, he was an empathetic guy...others had said so in the past. And she'd seen it, too. She's in a tight spot, already telling him things she'd not confided in others. Maybe he had an obligation to guide her through this. Maybe?

"Erica, you've had a lot to drink. So have I. You shouldn't have even tried to drive yourself home, much less over here. Neither of us should be driving. We need to call you a ride, so you can make it home safely."

She tossed her ebony mane and glanced around. "This is a big place. I assume you have a..."

"Or you can stay here in our guest quarters. I think it's made up." Truth was, he knew it was always prepared, courtesy of Margo and their weekly housekeeper. "Let me show you there. We both need to call it a night and get some rest." He needed to be the voice of reason here.

"Sounds great. Again, thank you. You're so thoughtful." She slid off the barstool, ready to be shown to the guest room.

Negotiating the wide hall off the kitchen and hearth room, they arrived at a suite of rooms near the back of the house, the master wing tucked away at the opposite end of the main floor. He flipped the light switch, and stepped back, allowing her to enter.

Quickly scanning the quarters, she turned to him. "This is lovely, really."

He smiled and pointed to the atrium doors at the far end of the room. "That opens onto a part of the back deck. I'll set the alarm when I go to bed, so I wouldn't open that during the night if I were you."

"No problem. I won't be sitting outside tonight, I'm sure."

"And there's the adjoining bath."

She glanced at the door he indicated and nodded.

Finished with his orientation, he said, "All right. I'll say goodnight, then."

He stepped into the hall and pulled closed the door.

Making his way through the kitchen again and into the main hall, he killed various lights as he went, satisfied he'd controlled the situation better than expected.

He wasn't sure where he was at that moment, but somewhere familiar, talking to a group of men. Colleagues, maybe some of them, but was it a medical meeting? Some wore frowns, some laughed, but had he made some sort of joke? He looked down and saw a drink in his hand. A very large drink, not his usual pour. And very colorful floral shorts girding his loins. Where did he get those? And Margo wasn't at his side. He'd apparently lost track of her. He glanced around, but the men gathered near him kept talking, wanting his attention. They were to leave the next day, or that had been the plan, but where was she? Was he going to leave without her, if she didn't materialize? The breezes caressed his face, and he looked out at the sunset over the Pacific horizon. Of course, they were in Maui...he knew that.

A warm hand grazed his back. His thoughts shifted, coming into blurry focus. What kind of room was he in? Things seemed out of whack. The window was on the wrong wall. He then realized he was in his own bed, his own house, and it was dark. This was not Maui. He must have been dreaming...

He turned over at the second touch, this time on his thigh. He felt warmth, pressure building. The scent swept over him, a scent he'd experienced before, just recently. Aroused then, he reached out, connected with soft, smooth skin and scant silk material, and suddenly realized a woman, a nearly naked woman was in bed with him. *Margo, come home?*

Before he could pull away, or regroup, she threw a leg over his, and melded her body against him, stroking his neck and shoulders, her soft breasts pressing his chest. He sensed he was awake, but floated in another world, inundated in his own desire. He wanted her, right then. There was no turning back.

TWELVE

Saturday

Ash stared out the large kitchen windows, his hands pressed to the cold granite countertop, a steaming cup of coffee waiting for his attention. The morning sun was too damn bright. A headache nagged – lack of sleep and too much alcohol – not a feel-good formula. He could think of nothing else except the turn of his night. How could he have been so stupid? He'd walked right down the path she'd blazed for him. Talk about vulnerable...him, not her.

Ash left his bed before six that morning, relieved the day had finally dawned. Locking his bathroom door, he blasted himself with as hot a shower as he could stand, hoping to wash away all residua of his failure, and of her. What had possessed him? Lust, weakness, genetics? Dumb question...he knew what.

When they'd collapsed after the frantic round of bed scrambling, she'd tried to snuggle at his side, wanting to talk. Fully awake then, but wishing he could succumb to sleep, he had forced himself to remain alert, and not encourage any cuddling. She had apologized, explained herself, and generally sought his sympathy for her unpredictable actions.

'She had never'...which he seriously doubted. But he registered his share of regrets for loss of control, as well. Finally, they quit with the apologies and pushed apart. So awkward. Silently staring at the ceiling, hands stacked behind his head, Ash found himself lost in thought and regret.

But Erica, sitting up and clutching her knees, had selected that moment to launch into a tragic story of a young woman, a close friend, who'd died of ovarian cancer complications. She'd been with her toward the end, and in the moment when she'd suffered a sudden respiratory arrest, Erica had attended to her, horrified when the code team arrived and undertook a useless resuscitation, despite her friend's wishes otherwise. Unfortunately, no other family members were present at that exact moment, and the team would not heed Erica's objections, newly-minted doctor that she was, regarding her friend's stated plans for withdrawal of care. She obviously felt she'd failed her friend, and now suspected that ordeal had energized her passion for end-of-life issues.

Ash, realizing this personal reveal went to the heart of the matter for this woman, refrained from questions or commentary. Moved by her description and true sadness, he was not about to cut her off and send her packing...dawn would come soon enough. He did suggest – more than suggest – that she return to the guest room for the remains of the night. She had agreed and padded away. And, he had locked his door. *Why didn't I think of that to begin with?*

His cell chimed. A call from the ICU at the hospital. Yes, he was on call that weekend, and yes, he would come in to consult on this new patient in acute renal and respiratory failure, someone they'd never seen before. He'd be there shortly.

He took a gulp of the cooling coffee, and turned when he heard movement behind him. It was not Roberta. He'd already let her out, fed her, and she'd taken up her usual position in the hearth room, watching him. She knew.

"Good morning," Erica offered. She now wore a small

63

blanket she'd found at the foot of the guest bed. Presumably, she'd donned her lingerie again and not left them in his room.

"Morning. Look…"

"No, don't say anything. It was all my doing. And I'm sorry…but not really sorry. You understand."

He wished he did. "I've got to go in. The ICU called. Someone's waiting."

"Sure."

"So, we both need to get going. I can't leave you here."

"Of course. I'll scoot."

"There's some coffee if you want." He indicated the fresh pot he'd made during his earlier ruminations.

"Thanks. I'll just be a few minutes." She reached for a mug he'd left out, and made her way to the back hall toward the guest room, where her discarded clothes lay strewn about.

Ash watched her disappear, then hustled to the master bedroom to make sure every trace of her had been removed. He'd make the bed and straighten up after he had the new patient taken care of and returned home. Spending time on that now was not a priority. *Surely I'll get back before Margo arrives.* Scanning the room, he saw nothing out of order. It was going to be bad enough when he came home and confronted the guilty feelings still hanging around, waiting there to pester him. No way did he want to pick up some woman's panties while he argued with himself, or those specters.

He returned to the hearth room, petted Roberta and said his goodbye, then onto the mudroom, to make sure she had all the food and water she'd need for the day, if he was detained.

Erica appeared in the doorway.

"Ready?" he asked, keeping a safe distance.

"Yes."

As they parted ways in the garage, she exited toward her vehicle in the driveway, looking composed and walking tall. He started his SUV's engine and sat, making sure she actually left the property, and his neighborhood. He'd bring up the rear. God, he was glad there weren't adjacent neighbors able to survey the front of his property.

As Ash approached the first corner, he paused, saw Erica take the curve away from him and his environs, and breathed a sigh of relief. *You are so thoroughly compromised,* a little voice reminded him.

At the first stoplight several miles down the road, a thought intruded. *Did I put that extra coffee cup in the dishwasher before I beat it out of there?*

THIRTEEN

The moment the garage door began its slow climb, her car tires came into view. Like two unexpected legs hiding behind draperies, where they weren't supposed to be. She was home, and his opportunity to spruce up had vanished. His empty stomach clenched and churned, any hope of a quiet lunch and much-needed introspection now evaporated.

Ash plastered a smile on his face – he would have to become a very good actor instantaneously – and turned the key in the lock. Inside the mudroom he took note first of her carryon sitting there, taunting him, waiting for his assistance. He moved through the space and into the large central hall, where Margo met him, Roberta at her side. They stopped in place, and smiled at him. Both of them.

"You're home," he said, hoping to convey enthusiasm, not disappointment or terror.

"Yes. Just a short while ago. So, you had to go in early." It was not a question. Those would come soon enough.

"Yeah, early. New dialysis patient, unexpectedly, and rounds."

"I wondered. Roberta gave me a tour of the place when I

66

arrived."

The Golden grinned. *You are so busted, buddy.*

Dizziness nearly overcame him as a sudden thought pierced. Had the lovely Erica tidied the guest quarters before she exited? He'd forgotten to check that little knotty detail.

She and Roberta took a step, changed direction, and made their way to the kitchen. Together. Over her shoulder, she remarked, "It looked like you were up and down all night. Lots of emergency patients?"

"Some, yes." *Erica wasn't exactly a patient, but she definitely constituted an emergency.*

He redirected immediately. "So, you got a lot done this week? The client pleased?"

Turning to the Keurig, she made herself a quick cup of coffee, and pivoted to him, Roberta plastered at her side. Margo's gaze felt a bit too deliberate, his guilty thoughts told him.

"Yes. It went well. We got off to a fast start early in the week, and the plans we'd formulated came together quickly. He liked everything, no debating, and we got the orders in."

"Sounds great." Why was the dog in full protective mode? She should have taken to the couch by then. He felt her warm brown gaze as well.

Margo sipped from her steaming cup, and squinted at him over the rim. "Yeah, I think it will be a good partnership over the long run."

Just how much of a partnership is she referring to? But he was in no position to question her, he realized, mentally slapping himself. "That sounds promising for their expansion."

"Believe so," she agreed, placing her mug on the counter and making her way to the powder room. "Think I'll go unpack, if you could carry my bag into the master closet for me, hon."

"Got it." *Hon*

What had he been thinking that morning, other than his wife wouldn't show up and confront the mess before he did?

He'd turned into a real dumb-ass over this stupid situation, and this corner he'd backed into was getting tighter and tighter. *When one lives with an interior designer for the better part of thirty years, one should remember that they keep an organized, done up house.* No unmade beds in the morning, revealing very used sheets – looking like some sort of scramble had occurred during the night – and no towels strewn here and there. No, Margo had changed the sheets before her Monday morning departure. She well knew what the bed looked like when only he slept there. And she had him very well trained. He felt the corner closing in, like some bad horror movie with the walls, ceiling, and floor shifting.

He made it to the closet, deposited the bag, and returned to the bedside, barely in time to smooth the sheets and blanket into place before she appeared.

"I think I'll just wash those sheets, and put on clean ones. These looked fairly used. Will you help me?"

"Sure." *After I go throw up...*

"Then I'd like to get on with my day. I have some work to do in the studio."

The bed stripped, and clean sheets installed, Margo gathered the soiled linens and prepared to bundle the whole wad to the laundry room. Stopping at the door, with Roberta at her heels, she gave him an over-the-shoulder look and informed him of another task.

"And would you pick up the guest room, too?"

The dog smiled at him, as if to say, 'Yeah, buddy,' before she loped along after her mistress.

FOURTEEN

Sunday

There wasn't enough grace in that place, or perhaps the entire world, to cover him. That thought would not leave Grant Ashton Meyers as he sat shoulder to shoulder with Margo, and other parishioners, and endured the Presbyterian service. It didn't help that they'd sat so close to the pulpit, enabling the pastor to keep him in his sights. Why hadn't they just slipped into a back pew?

They had awakened early that morning. Drifting off the night before beside his fabulous wife had calmed his nerves somewhat, although he'd begged off any intimate activity due to fatigue and call – not the weekend he'd envisioned just a short six days ago. But having her there reassured him. Strangely, it felt as if she'd brought a protective shield home with her from Oklahoma.

When dawn came, he'd hoped they could enjoy a nice long breakfast on the covered terrace and ease into the day. But when she suggested going to church that morning – after all, they hadn't been in about a month – his heart and soul sank. Did she know? Was this her way of punishing him, or was she turning him over to the Lord? If so, he wasn't in any bargaining position, and would just have to repent, beg for forgiveness, and endure.

Perseverance builds character, right? That was somewhere in scripture, he was sure, but where? And, he had hardly persevered, had he? Meanwhile, no doubt, he was headed toward a confession to his wife. Which could be cleansing, but the outcome was not guaranteed, so he'd think about that for a while. Hopefully, he would sense the right timing. Oh, man, this was so bad.

Interrupting his thoughts, a familiar-sounding passage rang out, 'For what I want to do I do not do, but what I hate I do.' The minister, quoting directly from Romans 7, looked straight at him. *Ouch!* This sermon was beyond timely. Had the clergy and Margo colluded? Thoroughly chastened, he silently prayed heaven would shower mercy upon him, and soon.

The last hymn sung, the benediction pronounced, he felt slightly relieved, smiled at Margo, and turned to greet those friends and acquaintances seated near them. But what was behind that sly smile directed his way? Did they suspect, or God forbid, know? Was his depravity so obvious?

The whole mortifying period over and chatting completed, he restrained himself from fleeing to the parking lot as if under duress. Appearing relaxed was key, but shaking hands with the minister was to be avoided. Of course, his apparent tension could always be attributed, if necessary, to call duties. And no sleep.

Not fifteen minutes later, they motored along a major thoroughfare, both lost in thought. Margo suddenly spoke. "Why don't we stop for brunch? We don't need a reservation at First Watch."

"Okay, sure."

It would at least forestall any more uncomfortable conversations which might arise in the confines of their home. He knew Margo would not broach any such subject in a public place. She just didn't do that type of thing. At least, not up until then. There was always a first time for everything, though, right?

He pulled into an open spot and killed the engine. Before either spoke, he jumped out and opened her door. Chivalry always pays off, too...or, it convicts you.

"I need to finish a couple of things in my studio. Would you take care of the bills, and put a call in to Cole? We haven't heard from him in a while."

She sailed through the kitchen and down the stairs to their lower level. Thank God for a small reprieve. But this ignoring of her obvious observations was enough to drive him crazy. Maybe that was her method. Doling out his punishment with a thousand little kindnesses, and requests. He wasn't sure, but he'd do as she asked.

Settled then in their library, the one place Erica's fingerprints weren't likely to be found, felt somewhat safe and relieving. But just as he finished the few bills due soon and picked up his cell to text his eldest son, a wave of guilt washed over him. How could he speak with either son while envisioning himself on Friday night? His betrayal stared him in the face just as plain as if it stood across the desk from him. Their mother was a great woman. And they loved her immensely, and she, them. A woman he had deceived.

Then, without warning, his father's image appeared, reminding him – like father, like son? The abandonment, the hurt, had apparently never left him, no matter the time interval or how hard he'd worked to suppress it. Using various women for pleasure alone, finally running off with one of them, leaving his mother, his sister, and him to figure it out and forge their own way. Which they had done quite well. All of them, in fact.

Some would say Ash had spent considerable time and energy overcompensating, excelling at anything he put his mind to. And along the way he had vowed as a teenager he would never treat a wife and children in like manner. So, here it stood – his guilt – taunting him. Did he possibly possess a heritable condition, something in his genes? Nonsense. But was this what he had to live with now, every day? His revealed weakness, not to mention the shame and guilt. There was no escape, and certainly there were no excuses. That was obvious.

He punched in a quick text message to Cole and tried to focus on ignored emails. He startled when his cell chimed. It was not his son, but the hospital informing him of another new renal consult.

Hallelujah! He could escape...albeit, temporarily. Dive into medicine, do something right.

FIFTEEN

Monday

He crested the top of the open staircase and noted her secretary smiling as he approached. "I have an appointment with Ms. Nelson," he informed her.

"Yes, she's expecting you. Please be…"

Kristine Nelson's door opened, and she silently beckoned Ash with a gesture. He noticed she wore a navy sheath and heels, minimal jewelry again, which called attention to the giant rock on her right hand. She appeared dressed for some serious administrating that day.

Once in and the door closed, she greeted him. "How are you this morning?"

He wasn't sure, but said, "Fine."

She resumed her seat behind her faux mahogany desk and smiled. "Thank you for coming on such short notice. You must have rounds to finish."

"Yes, and several of the new patients require dialysis. It's busy this week."

"Yes, I'm aware." She gazed at him, then said, "I called you in to follow up our discussion of last week, regarding the situation with Dr. Lange. Several points you made stimulated

73

further thought."

Was he ever going to be able to lay Dr. Erica Lange aside? Apparently not. "Some thoughts?"

"Yes. I'm sure you've had a chance to review the withdrawal of care policy I sent you, and wondered if you had any opinions you'd like to share?"

"I looked it over the middle of last week," – *and boy, have I had an active five-day interval* – "and basically felt it looked in order. There is some indefinite language, but it doesn't seem to wrest control of DNR counseling from the doctors."

"I don't think so either."

"That would certainly concern me, as I said last Tuesday. And any intrusion or interference with independent medical decision-making by the doctors here. So, thoughts you had?"

She shifted, then re-established eye contact. "Well, since we spoke, I wondered how Dr. Lange was doing, and whether you believed her story about the nurses?"

"She seems to be doing fine, as far as I know." *As of Saturday morning.* "As to the nurses keeping track of her discussions with patients, or spying as she put it, I don't know. I don't have any more information on that."

Wearing a concerned look, Kristine asked, "When you spoke with her, did she seem to have specific evidence of that activity?"

Okay, what was Kristine fishing for? Had Erica already called corporate? How could she have had time since Friday evening? Well, it was ten A.M. Monday morning. Maybe she was an early riser. Of course, with two children…"I haven't seen any evidence."

Kristine's face relaxed a fraction. "I confess, it's worried me a bit that perhaps some of our staff was engaged in monitoring her unduly, or inappropriately. I'm sure you know, we wouldn't encourage such a thing. At least, not myself nor Ric Newman. That wouldn't be professional." Serious then, she leaned forward over the desk edge. "I'd certainly want you to inform me of such behavior if you, or your colleagues, notice nurses behaving that way toward any of you."

"All right." He paused, then said, "One thing I would suggest...perhaps you should have legal review your policy, revise any vague language, and provide staff in-service education regarding the wording and the spirit of the policy. Maybe it's a matter of understanding among some of the staff."

She smiled broadly. "I like your thinking and your suggestion. That's excellent."

"Thanks." He glanced at the clock directly above her head.

"Well," she said, standing abruptly from her chair, "that's about all I wanted to discuss. I do hope we'll stay in touch. And I *will* call legal and broach the subject of a policy review. I appreciate you suggesting that." She rounded her desk and offered her hand. They shook and he turned to leave.

When he cleared the door, she again reminded him to keep in touch, then retreated into her inner sanctum.

Ash beat it down the stairs, proceeding directly to another wing of patients. He would immerse himself in clinical care that day. Perhaps for just a few hours he could forget the enchanting Dr. Lange.

But not the just-completed discussion which seemed laden with unspoken agenda.

~ ~ ~ ~

Kristine Nelson didn't resume her seat and dive into the mundane paperwork littering her desk. She gazed out her office windows, wondering what her next move would be. And who she should align with.

This Dr. Meyers was a straight-up guy, a person of integrity – her gut told her that – who appeared concerned only with quality patient care and staying on the right side of an issue. But he also cared about doctor autonomy, had

75

repeatedly mentioned it. That might get sticky. And he'd, at first, seemed rather protective of Dr. Lange. Today, however, she hadn't detected any of that undo concern for his former colleague. There had been one moment, though, when she'd asked him how Erica was doing, and noticed his eyes flicker, his face tense. He'd looked eager to get on with it and get out of there. She'd sensed that much. Perhaps the two had stayed in touch a bit more since last Tuesday than he let on.

Kristine turned back to her desk and dropped into the chair. It was time to regroup, decide how to proceed from here. Straddling the fence was always an uncomfortable position to maintain for long. Was it time to consider switching sides?

Her secretary rapped and simultaneously opened the door.

"Yes, what is it?" she snapped, then regretted her sharp tone.

"May I get you anything from the lounge, ma'am?"

"Some strong black coffee, if you would. I could use the boost. Unless there's something stronger you'd suggest?"

~ ~ ~ ~

June sat, headset in place, discussing appointments with a patient when Ash rounded the corner and moved directly into his office. It was late, and he needed to finish several dictations from the weekend before heading home.

Finished, she stuck her head in the door, "Need anything before I leave?"

"No, I'm good."

He forced a smile, and she observed, "You must have had a really busy day."

"Yeah, it was."

"You coming in tomorrow?"

"Probably after I finish rounds."

"Okay, see you then."

June had just stepped aside when a younger medical

76

assistant materialized behind her and, wearing a broad smile, poked her head in the door. Holding his headset, he gave her a quizzical look.

"Was that you I saw at the Chisholm Grill Friday night with your gorgeous wife?" She added a wink.

Stunned, Ash gripped the device tighter and nodded, fearing he'd squeak if he spoke. Or crush, maybe mangle, the thing in his hand.

"I thought that was you, but I've never seen your wife. You'll have to bring her to the Christmas party this year, so we can all meet her. She's very beautiful."

That she is, but you've got the wrong woman. God almighty.

She gazed at him for a long moment. There was no doubt his expression could raise concern in anyone. And if his lunch hadn't been consumed so long ago, he was sure he could reproduce it on the spot.

"Are you okay, Dr. Meyers? You look funny. Can I get you something?"

He cleared his throat, and rasped, "No, I'm fine. Just need some water." He dropped his headset, grabbed the water bottle, and took a generous gulp. Damp down the reflux brash, or anything else threatening to erupt.

Looking dubious, she said, "Well, all right, see you tomorrow," and slipped away from his door.

He waited a moment, then rose and closed his office door. His heart pounded, and a fullness he couldn't suppress rose in his neck, threatening his vision and his upright posture. No more interruptions, no more terrifying announcements permitted. This was a nightmare! He needed to wake up and seize control of this situation immediately. He fell into his chair and stared at his computer screen.

And that process had to begin at home.

Sixteen

Tuesday

Chase Monroe stared at the email. Though short, the message was clear. They had developed a big problem in Kansas City. And it was expanding.

What exactly had gone wrong with this crusading doctor? Kristine Nelson outlined the basics last Thursday, making her case for their vulnerability. Which he hadn't wanted to believe, at first. Surely, they could do something to arrest any further progress, especially if she, the doctor, went off the rails. They – well, he – had to, before the CEO got wind of this. Even though their strategy could not be specifically pinned to his covert planning, nor any other person's, he now feared his methods may have been discovered and could be scrutinized, opening the door to regulatory remedies, or worse.

This Dr. Lange – who exactly was she? He hadn't wanted to know too much about her. And her apparent ally, what's his name? He glanced at the notes he'd taken while Kristine had given him the run-down. Yes, there it was, Dr. Meyers, Grant Ashton Meyers. He'd look him up and see how worthy an opponent he might be.

Ignoring his other work, Chase poked around on the internet, found Dr. Meyers name, and clicked on the link to his practice. His heart sank. The all-American boy stared back at him. And on the next page, there stood his sharp-looking eight-person group – four pulmonologists, two nephrologists, including Meyers, one neurologist, and one cardiologist – all board certified in intensive care as well as their respective subspecialties, all with years of experience under their belts. Men and women with impeccable credentials. Absolutely not a bunch he'd want to cross, or challenge, in front of regulators or lawyers. Not to mention they needed such doctors to help staff their facilities, and to bring substance and status to their operation.

He closed the link and stared into near space. Yes, it was time to shift gears, cool it a bit with the plan, and prepare an excellent defensive strategy. They may have just gotten a little carried away with their initiative, that's all.

~ ~ ~ ~

This time when the garage door rose, Margo's car wasn't waiting. Ash breathed a sigh of relief. He could get inside, take care of Roberta's needs, and prepare to confront the situation, and himself, when she arrived.

When he opened the back door, Roberta let loose with one bark, bounded into the mudroom, and jumped up with her greeting. "Good girl, good girl," Ash praised her, petting her head. "You're my pal, aren't you? Let's go." The dog smiled, but then she always did.

The back door gaping open, out she ran. While Roberta checked the property and took care of business, he'd take the short hike to their mailbox, and be done with it. Scanning the surrounding woods as he went, he felt reassured and relieved Erica wasn't lurking amongst the trees, waiting for him. Maybe she had finally given up. Still, he needed to come clean with Margo. He couldn't live this way, and she didn't deserve his deception.

He met Roberta again on the driveway as she bounded around the garage corner, and inside they went. The sun was setting on what had been a beautiful fall day, and dusk was creeping in. Nightfall and Margo would arrive soon.

"Oh, how nice. You've gotten dinner ready. And a glass of wine, too." Margo observed upon entering the kitchen and scanning the scene. She smiled, "Thanks, darling."

I am no darling. "It was the least I could do with you working late." *And with what I'm about to lay on you.* "That's usually my situation."

"Let me dump these things in the studio, and I'll be right back up." And off she went to the lower level, the dog at her heels.

He took a deep breath and expelled it on a huff. This was not going to be easy, and he cautioned himself not to guzzle too much wine. He had his well-rehearsed speech in mind, and no matter how it went, dinner and it would be over within the next two hours. They'd either be hoarse from shouting, or he'd be out on the front step, bag in hand. There weren't too many other options that he could foresee. Unless, maybe…

Margo sat on one loveseat, he on its mate, facing each other across the near void, and the large glass cocktail table. She sipped her remaining wine and regarded him. Their dinner and cleanup now history, he'd suggested relaxing in the hearth room.

Thus situated, wine glasses in hand, he'd begun with a summary recap of the situation thrust upon him a mere ten days before. And its swift progress since. How long ago that seemed. With Margo sufficiently warmed up to the predicament, he'd then briefly reported what had happened Friday evening and night. Kept it to the point. She'd remained impassive, sipping wine throughout his crisp confession, and then spoke.

"I knew things were out of whack Saturday. That shouldn't surprise you. It was obvious something had gone on. But it was your story to tell."

"What if I hadn't said anything?"

"That's not the point now, but I had my strategies mapped out. You would not have fared well." That he knew. This woman was poised, if anything, and meant what she said.

Apparently desiring repeat clarification, she asked, "So, tell me again, when did this all start?"

"Only last Wednesday."

Margo's brow rose, her expression dubious.

"Well, actually the Friday before, when I came upon her in the doctors' office at Oakwood, crying."

"So, a crying woman can carry you off to bed inside of one week? That's rather flimsy."

Apparently, so. She had him there. He shrugged. "I can't defend my actions."

"How true, but I don't care for your shrug. She must be one convincing chick."

His energy suddenly sapped, he withered under his wife's stare.

She then asked, "So, what do you propose doing now about this mess?"

"Fix it with you. I love you, Margo, and I don't want my loss of control on one occasion to ruin our relationship. We have something here – we've built our life together – and it doesn't deserve to be trashed by my actions."

"You're right that our marriage didn't deserve what you did. I need to know, though, what about her and this situation drew you in?"

He took a breath, summoned the remaining shred of courage he had, and launched into the summary of what had happened on or about Friday, October eleventh and forward. It didn't take long. Margo didn't interrupt, except to refocus him when he strayed into talking about the underlying issue affecting Erica, her employment, and care withdrawal at Oakwood.

She rightfully corrected him that those were two separate

issues; he should not confuse the two. Just because he felt sorry for Erica's situation, and had agreed in principle with her, that was no reason to share a bed with the woman. No matter how gorgeous or persistent she was.

"How do you feel about her now?"

"Negative. And I did, right away."

"That's only a little reassuring. Are you sure?"

"Absolutely."

"All right...because what I'm going to suggest won't be easy for you. Or me. Hopefully, not her either."

He regarded his wife with relief, and a good measure of anxiety. But, what was she about to suggest or demand?

Within minutes Margo had outlined her plan, one they would implement together. The caveat – if he muffed it, he was out of there. And she'd keep the house, the dog, a good bit of their shared money, and rearrange their sons' thinking.

He believed her.

SEVENTEEN

Thursday

The corner they'd chosen was out of the way, and the tall booth they occupied offered well-padded sides all around. But it still afforded a view of the front reception area. They would not be bothered there by other patrons, and they had instructed the wait staff to give them some time. Their needs would be minimal. Ash and Margo waited, sipping their weak drinks.

Considerable discussion had transpired between the two of them since Tuesday evening when she had outlined their plan. He could hardly argue, having demonstrated no planning prowess and having lost complete control of the situation. And Margo's strategy made perfect sense. Erica herself had unwittingly facilitated the scheduling of the get-together when she contacted Ash by text on Wednesday, wishing to meet and bring him up to date on her 'options'. He'd told her things had changed but had not admitted that he had confessed anything to his wife.

Only fifteen minutes after the appointed time, Ash saw Erica sail through the huge door of the bar and glance around. He touched Margo's hand, alerting her to the doctor's arrival.

Margo immediately oriented in that direction. A low 'hum' vibrated from her throat when she sighted Erica, the opponent. She squeezed his hand, released it, and took another sip. The message: man your stations.

There was no doubt Erica came dressed for the occasion, her full black mane swinging free as she approached – sweater and slacks in warm fall hues, tall leather boots, and her slouchy shoulder bag. Large loop earrings hung from nearly concealed earlobes – earlobes he knew quite well – sheltered by her massive mane, and not too much makeup this time. He knew Margo, in full observation mode, was sizing up her style. With a show of manners, Ash stood, awaiting her arrival at their booth. However, there would be no hand shaking, no touching at all.

Brief, crisp introductions completed, Erica took a seat across from the pair. Ash noted she worked to conceal her surprise at Margo's presence, observing her subtle regard and assessment of his wife. Margo held her own, unflinching. Time to move on. And it didn't seem appropriate to waste time in small talk and smiling, so Ash began...as per Margo's plan.

"We appreciate you meeting with us this evening."

Erica gazed at them and nodded. "Sure, and I am glad to meet with you."

Likely only referring to Ash, though. Was she trying to figure out if Margo knew about the hot encounter last Friday? He wasn't sure if or when he would clue her in that Margo knew, and that she – his wife – was a major player in whatever happened next. He'd try to fit it in somewhere, depending on the course of this conversation, or how presumptuous Erica became during the discussion.

"You contacted me yesterday about options you've developed, and said you wished to update me on the progress you've made about your termination."

"That's right."

"So, why don't you give us that information now?"

Glancing between the two of them, Erica hesitated.

"Margo's been updated." His wife smiled pleasantly. No big deal, right?

Erica shrugged and straightened her spine. With a confident air and a toss of her head, she began. "I explained I might pursue a wrongful termination action. And I'm still going in that direction."

"Have you consulted with a labor lawyer?"

"Not yet. I'm waiting to hear back. Basically, they can't terminate a doctor for taking good care of patients and doing what's right in the clinical situation. That would apply to all of us, right?"

"Get some legal advice, Erica."

She threw him a scornful look and went on. "I told you before about the incentives we know the nurses, and others, are given for pressuring patients to change their DNR orders, or reporting discussions we have with patients and families to encourage them to reconsider DNR. That much we've already discussed."

Ash nodded.

She went on, "And I told you I would get evidence of that through my sources."

"What are your sources? Raina Crawford?"

"No, not just Raina. I'll get to that in a minute." She paused when their waitperson approached, allowing her to order a glass of wine. When he retreated, she continued, "I've looked into which department in the state, or federal, bureaucracy I should contact. About the fraud and probable corruption."

"What particulars point to fraud, exactly?"

"Paying staff to keep heads in the beds. Keeping people alive for profit." He could see Margo's steady gaze in his peripheral vision, was glad he'd equipped her with all the phraseology and lingo they might throw around. "Whether they paid them bonuses, or in-kind with continuing education, all that."

"Okay, so I advised you to seek legal counsel if you wished to move forward. Have you gotten an opinion yet?"

"I said, not yet. No. But that's coming."

"You seem very sure of your position. And you've asked me at times to back up your efforts. So, who are your sources?"

She smiled at him. "Raina and I have both made observations of our own, but there are a few staff members who've been cut out of the incentives, who've come to us and complained."

"Will you be more specific?"

"I don't think I should, since you still go there and interact with some of them."

"Generically, then..."

"Generically, one of the social workers and a few nursing staff."

"Any administrative assistants?"

"I don't know for sure."

"The Director of Nursing? Or the chief administrator Kristine Nelson?"

"I'll not say."

Or you don't know. Was he to believe that Kristine Nelson or Ric Newman were in on some grand scheme to maintain occupancy and further billing? Or were Kristine and Ric playing both sides? Perhaps, Kristine's two meetings with him were part of a larger well-orchestrated strategy. Or was this woman sitting across from him lying or completely off her rocker?

"Since you're not attending there anymore...so, let me clarify, I assume you mean you're still getting information through Raina? And others who inform you?"

"You could say that."

"Okay, look Erica, I believe this has escalated to a level I cannot support any further. And, if all you say is true, there's really nothing I can do which will take it down, or reverse what the parties there have done or may do."

"I beg to differ. I believe a physician such as yourself, or others in your practice, carry more weight than you may think. Your awareness and possible intervention could mean a great deal to this effort."

"That won't restore your position with the medicine group." He hoped his facial expression matched his firm words. "I must remind you, this is your effort. I hadn't joined the team yet when this all spun out of control. And my group is not going to jump into this mess with both feet."

Fired up, and apparently not registering what meaning his words held, she retorted, "Perhaps not. But it is the right thing to do, and I can't believe you would let something like this slide. You will not deter me from proceeding, if that's what you thought this conversation would accomplish. For your information..." She paused, glancing between Ash and Margo. "I have already contacted the state hospital association and CMS regarding my evidence."

"That's a big step, Erica, and one I suggest you obtain legal assistance with. You're wading into fairly deep water."

She sat quietly, sipping her wine, and regarded them. He suspected she wanted badly to know what Margo knew. Would she suddenly burst forth with their sordid little story? It would likely be far more colorful than the one he'd laid on Margo.

Finally, she admitted, "Perhaps I am."

~ ~ ~ ~

"She's quite a number."

Ash didn't think a confirmation or refutation was in order. His wife's observational skills were highly developed, and he would never distrust nor dispute them. The woman saw color and pattern, not to mention texture, where he saw nothing.

She turned slightly in her seat and looked at him. "I can see why you had a problem with her."

Good, she's on my side.

"But that doesn't excuse any of your actions. I would hope you could resist such obvious manipulation."

Not going to give me a pass.

87

"And keep it in your pants."

Ouch! Tough talk.

The remainder of their discussion with Erica had not produced further insight on her part, that he could see, anyway. She persisted in espousing her absolute justifiable position. What did she think she'd gain? He couldn't figure it out. And after reiterating her findings, her suspicions, and her desire to push forward, they had agreed to quit discussing it. He'd made it clear he wasn't just temporarily suspending the conversation to reconvene another day. That it was over from his perspective, and there was nothing further he could or would do. He'd said it so many times already, he was sure he sounded like a broken record.

"Obviously, I didn't. And I'm ashamed to have fallen for that."

"What do you think she's going to do?"

"Other than what she said, I don't know. I originally encouraged her to look around, seek a position with another group. With the two kids, I'm sure she has to work."

"Unless she's gotten a lot of money out of that ex-husband."

"True. But I'm worried she's gone off the deep end, and with the kids...what a mess," he said, taking a corner into their development.

"I'm less sympathetic than you. I'll remind you, she's a grown woman, nearly forty years old, a doctor for God's sake, and a mother. She should always keep her kids' well-being in mind. And she's the custodial parent." They pulled into their long drive and approached the house. "Have you considered that she may be on the take herself? Looking for some settlement from a lawsuit or as a whistle-blower?"

"You may have a point," he said, pulling into the garage alongside her car.

"And I'd watch my own back, too, if I were you. You may end up implicated if she doesn't like your discharging her and her crusade this evening. You know, a woman scorned..."

Margo got out and walked straight to the back door. Roberta was waiting.

Struck by her comment, he didn't immediately jump from his SUV.

Had he, in fact, just created two scorned women? What a perilous position to find oneself in.

EIGHTEEN

Friday

She hated leaving voice messages. No telling when someone would return the call, if ever. It was Friday, after all. That woman at CMS had taken and now held all the information she had relayed to her, and she didn't want to retell her story to a different person every time she called. Erica furiously tapped in another email to Helen Ramsey's private box, hit send, and opened up another window.

There was his picture. Ashton Meyers, MD, smiling at her. The doctor was sure a hunk of a man, at least in her estimation. Tall, sandy blond hair – in fact, sandy hair everywhere which she couldn't wipe from her memory – and broad shoulders, strong arms and legs, good hands...My God, she needed to stop this!

"He has a wife," she reminded herself out loud, and a beautiful one at that. Margo Swafford Meyers was very smart, and certainly no fool. She wasn't going to kick him to the curb and into someone else's arms, even if she was a successful business owner in her own right. No, the woman would go to the mat for that man, she was sure of that. Erica smiled. So should any woman. She closed the page and rose from her desk. It was nearly noon.

She made it as far as her study door when her cell rang. It was Helen...wonderful!

Greetings aside, Ms. Ramsey acknowledged Erica had called and came directly to the point. "I understand you have additional information for me, Dr. Lange?"

"Yes, that's right."

"I'll take notes while we discuss, okay?"

Was she being recorded? Oh, what the hell..."Yes, that's fine."

"Go ahead."

"Last week when we spoke, I told you about my termination from the internal medicine group at Oakwood Specialty Hospital, a Chicago-based company that owns a number of long-term acute care facilities around the country. I also said I believe there is a scheme in that organization to maintain patients alive, beyond their reasonable expectation of meaningful life, for the purpose of excess billing." She paused when Helen cleared her throat. "Shall I go on?"

"Yes, please."

"And, I believe my unwillingness to act in accordance with that plan caused my termination. Now, I have more evidence to support that belief."

"Evidence." It was not a question.

"That's right. I've found out that some nurses and other personnel are paid bonuses or receive preferential treatment – you might say, paid in kind – for assisting or participating in that scheme."

"That's a serious charge, Doctor."

"Quite. And with regards to my employment by the internal medicine group there, these nurses and others spied on me and reported my discussions with patients and families."

There was silence on the other end.

"Ms. Ramsey, are you still there?"

"Yes. May I ask you a question?"

"Of course."

"So, who do these nurse spies and others report to? Who do you think is in charge of this alleged scheme?"

The woman conveyed a skeptical tone. On guard then, Erica curtailed her own shrillness. "I believe either the COO, but more likely the Director of Nursing and my former colleague, the head of the internal medicine group."

"That seems quite a few people, Dr. Lange, to be in charge of a secret scheme."

"Are you doubting me?"

"No, not necessarily. But you have to understand, we must thoroughly vet stories like this before we go poking around investigating directly. If what you say is true, it is a very serious charge, and one which may take some time to look into. Are you willing to give me the names of those individuals?"

"Yes, now if you like. And it isn't just a story."

"Yes, ma'am. And anyone else you may have told about this."

Erica smiled. "Okay, ready?"

"Yes, I have pen in hand."

"Kristine Nelson, COO. Ric Newman, Director of Nursing. And Todd Griswold, MD, head of Premier Medical Associates."

"And anyone else...?"

"Grant Ashton Meyers, MD, nephrologist and intensivist."

~ ~ ~ ~

"Wow, that woman's either vindictive, or she's holding real information that could sink that entire organization," Special Agent Robert Cline observed.

He sat, one hip propped on the corner of Helen's desk. She'd purposely waited to return Erica's call until she could arrange for an appropriate authority to be present and listen in. It was obvious from the first time the doctor had called that she was on a mission of some sort. Fraud and abuse, a corruption scheme, the whole nine yards. And if so, the FBI would also get involved.

"It is remarkable, really. We haven't had a call like that in a long time. If we could get around the drama, I might actually be inclined to believe it."

"Despite the messenger, we can't dismiss it out of hand. I'll look into her charges and get back to you. I'd advise you, in the meantime, to pursue your usual investigative course."

"Will do."

"And don't delay. This Dr. Lange sounds like a loose cannon."

~ ~ ~ ~

She slammed the door with a foot, balancing groceries in one arm, a wine bottle in the other, with a large leather bag pressing down on her right shoulder, adding pain to the whole process. Her cell vibrated and chimed deep within the shoulder bag, diverting her attention. Dropping the assorted packages on the counter, she answered.

"Hi there...I was just thinking of you." Though not in the way he might imagine.

"As was I...that's why I called, Kristine."

She paused. Should she have picked up, or waited to return his call, forcing him to leave a message? "It's getting late. Don't you have plans for the weekend?"

"Not particularly."

"Look, Harris, I just walked in and a bunch of groceries are waiting." Checking her sharp tone, she added, "Perhaps we should have this chat another time."

Kristine walked over to the kitchen counter and inspected the wet spot on a corner of one paper bag. Choosing instead to focus on her wine purchase, she tapped on speaker, rested the phone on her granite countertop, and proceeded to unsheathe the wine bottle. She plucked a glass from a cabinet, and poured herself a rather full portion. If this conversation were to go smoothly, she might need the help.

"Perhaps." He'd obviously been drinking, took a noisy

sip then went on, "When might I see you again?"

"Oh, God, Harry, I don't know. It's busy right now, and I can't possibly get away. You must be involved there, aren't you?"

Picking up her phone, she took it off speaker, walked to the opposite wall of windows in her condo and stared out into the early evening. She observed nearby twinkling lights springing to life, and below, couples populating the sidewalks, ducking into trendy restaurants and shops, ready for a full Friday evening. She took a generous sip of wine.

He avoided her question, redirected and asked, "How's Kansas City? You still like it there, don't you?"

"Of course. Yes, I do, very much better than Little Rock."

"That's good. I'm pleased. And the position? That's going well?"

"So well, I can hardly focus on anything else." *If you only knew.* Another sip of wine, and the desired warmth spread.

"Good, good. Say, this is short notice, but how about we plan something for next weekend? The wife is going out of town for a few days. I could come to KC. Or, why don't we fly to New York and meet? No problem there."

"That does sound exciting, Harry, but let me think about it over the weekend. All right? I may need to get together with my daughter. She has a parents' thing at Grinnell next week." She paused and took a sip. "I'll check with her by Sunday evening and let you know."

"I look forward to it, Kristine. Don't let me down. I like our little arrangement and don't want to be disappointed, you understand?"

How she did. She pivoted from the windows and caught sight of an expanding pool of something spreading from the grocery sack. "Oh, hey, listen, I have some frozen groceries melting on my counter. Gotta go. I'll call you Sunday evening, if that works."

"Use the other phone."

"Got it. Bye, Harris."

She disconnected before he could trap her with any more reminders, and raced to her kitchen. Pulling the lettuce and eggs from the top of the bag, she peered into the interior. Of course…the damaged Ben and Jerry's container had oozed its creamy contents all over her clean counter.

Not unlike this relationship she'd sought and fostered, oozing into all reaches of her now convoluted life.

NINETEEN

Saturday

He couldn't argue with what she'd said. Ash took a corner and pulled into the parking lot of the ubiquitous big box store. They needed a few things inside, then Margo wanted to visit the outdoor garden department for pumpkins and other fall perennials. His wife always had good advice, and didn't hesitate to dole it out, especially when they roamed around on errands. Talking while driving always made it easier anyway, took the heat off – not having to maintain eye contact with her while thinking.

"Well, we can't go on about this inside," he announced.

"Saved by the stop?"

He smiled. "I'm sure we'll resume shortly."

Having finished shopping and loading, they wound their way through the crowded parking lot, and onto the next major street before she spoke again.

"Really, Ash, it's time you spoke with Scott."

"Scott?"

"Feinstein. You need some lawyerly advice yourself."

"I thought about that once Thursday evening when I reminded Erica to seek legal counsel, then frankly shoved it

96

to the back burner yesterday."

"It's appropriate, Ash, and probably wise. He may refer you on to someone else, but at least get his opinion. He's never misled us on other questions we've had. And this is more than a question."

At the next stoplight, he glanced at her.

"Yes," she said, "I'm very concerned. That Dr. Lange is quite a piece of work. No telling what she might do next. Or what else she might drag you into."

Ash redirected his gaze forward as the light changed. His foot heavy on the accelerator, they leapt away from the light and sped through the intersection.

"Easy, big boy. You know I'm right."

She almost always was.

"In fact, you might also need a restraining order."

Crap!

"Just see what he says."

Yes, ma'am. "Fair enough."

~ ~ ~ ~

"Mommy, why are we driving around? I don't want to be in the car."

"Me either."

Erica glanced in the rearview mirror, smiled, and said in a perky voice, "Just a little drive around, before we pick up our food. Maybe we'll see some Halloween decorations. That'd be fun, right?"

"I want to go home," Riley whined.

Her backseat passengers quieted. She doubted, though, they shared any of her excitement. She'd better get to MacDonald's quick or she might have a mutiny on her hands and more than whining to contend with.

"Where are we, anyway?" daughter Riley asked.

"We're in a nice neighborhood with all these big houses where a friend of mine lives."

"Are you going to stop at your friend's house? Do they

97

have kids?" Reynolds asked.

"Not tonight, no."

"Why not?"

And, why hadn't she expected these questions? "Because we need to pick up dinner and get back home, right?"

No answer from the back. She had approached the Meyers' property and arriving at their long drive, she slowed a bit.

"Is this your friend's house?" Riley asked. "Look, they have a dog, mommy!"

Reynolds craned to look out his side window. "A big dog," he announced.

Oops! Hopefully, Roberta hadn't seen or heard her car yet, and wouldn't come running. Erica quickly glanced down the drive and caught a glimpse of Ash in the distance standing on the drive, thankfully not facing her direction. He'd likely recognize her red Toyota SUV if he spotted it. Roberta oriented toward the street and let out one loud bark. Erica stepped on the gas and proceeded straight, seeking the concealment of nearby tall pines along the road, and hoping to find another drive in which to turn around. Or, preferably another way out of the development.

"I want to see their dog," Reynolds implored.

"Not this evening, Rey. Maybe another time. Let's go. What do you all want from MacDonald's?"

The usual backseat discussion commenced about their respective orders. They then debated which food was best. And who was the stupidest when it came to what food they ate and what they thought, allowing Erica free thinking time.

She'd laid her plan out there for Helen Ramsey and CMS to chew on. There was no way they'd dismiss such a case of potential Medicare or Medicaid fraud and abuse. And the insurance companies involved would gnash at the bit to get in on the action. That would gobble up a good bit of time. This could even go the RICO route. And potentially pave the way for other types of opportunities.

But perhaps she shouldn't have given them Ash's name

as a witness or informed person. Did she really want to cause him harm? No, but hey, he was and is an informed person. He let himself in that office two weeks ago didn't he? And asked her questions? So, he couldn't expect to just skip from all this...she refused to let him off that easy.

Had he told Margo about them? It was hard to know from their encounter Thursday evening. Was he holding his wife up there like some clueless shield? He shouldn't. Not fair. A woman needs to know what's going on and the identity of her opponent. Fight fair and square.

"Stop touching me!" Riley yelled.

"Then don't call me stupid!" shouted young Reynolds.

Yes, it was time to send Mrs. Margo Swafford Meyers the pictures and video. Throw that out there and see what kind of response issues forth. Ash might find himself on the curb after all, needing warm arms to console him.

"Hey, Riley, Rey...stop that right now!"

She turned into the MacDonald's parking lot, and the backseat immediately fell silent.

TWENTY

Sunday

She couldn't believe what she was seeing. *When had this happened?* Margo gripped her cell phone and fell into a small club chair in their master suite. Ash had run a quick errand and would return in time for the mid-afternoon start of that week's NFL game. They'd planned a chili supper for later. But right then, she thought she might throw up.

Okay, she'd had enough! He'd had plenty of time to come clean and tell her all of what had transpired between him and that woman. No more of this. She rose, marched to their master closet, and yanked a suitcase from the shelf. She needed to get away and think. Now!

Ash walked through the mudroom and stopped. There sat Margo's packed carryon – sides bulging – waiting in the main hall. What on earth? She rounded the corner with Roberta in tow, and halted at the sight of him. She did not wear a smile.

He stood there holding the grocery bag, staring at her. "What's all this about?"

"I could ask you the same."

He gave her a quizzical look. She walked straight toward him, stuck out her arm, handing him her cell phone, as she breezed past. "Here, look at this."

"Look at what?"

"The pictures and video. You'll see," she yelled from the kitchen.

"Are the boys up to something?"

"Far from it, but their father is."

Stunned, Ash followed her to the kitchen, dropped the groceries on the counter, and stood scrolling through her cell until he came to the message from that day. Oh, my God! How had Erica gotten Margo's cell number?

Then he saw the attached still pictures. It looked like she'd stood by her car, snapped pictures of herself with their house in the background. Her attire looked familiar. Yes, it was from that Wednesday evening when she'd presumed to drop by, gosh over ten days ago.

Then he hit the video play icon.

His gut clenched. Erica standing there, taking a selfie, hair and makeup all messed up, an earring missing, huffing out her message about sexual harassment and assault. His vision constricted to a pinpoint as he found his way to the counter and dropped onto a bar stool. He barely made it. Staring at the screen, he couldn't believe what he was seeing, and replayed the short video over and over. What a lie! What a treacherous, lying bitch!

He glanced around. Margo had apparently gone to her basement studio, hopefully to return soon. He needed to grab control immediately. She was so right. He must call Scott Feinstein first thing tomorrow. Maybe tonight. Why wait?

Not ten minutes later, Margo returned from the lower level and stood behind the counter, toting a large portfolio of designs, looking calm and determined. She reached over and retrieved her cell phone from the counter where it lay.

Ash regarded her, but said nothing.

"Are you going to say anything, or just sit there mute?"

"There's a lot I could say. I'm stunned, for one. This is

fiction. You have to know, but how can I prove I'm telling the truth?"

"With what went on just forty-eight hours after that, I'm not sure that statement is plausible. Look, I told you that woman was trouble. The gloves come off with someone like that, but it sounds like you already have done that and more!"

He couldn't fault her for getting excited. This was stunning. And horrible. What else had Erica done? "Where are you going? I should be the one to leave, if either of us does."

"Perhaps you're right, but I'm departing, abandoning you to your problem, and checking in on a client. I don't know how long I'll be gone."

"The new client in Tulsa?"

"What do you care? A client. I'll be in touch when I want to." She turned on her heel and headed to the hall. "That should give you all kinds of time to consort with the lovely doctor."

He stood from the barstool and followed her into the mudroom. As she gripped the doorknob, he spoke. "Margo, please don't leave. We must work this out."

She bent down, gave Roberta a kiss on the head and rubbed her ears, but ignored his plea. She said, "Take a look at the next message I received. I forwarded those all to you. Good luck working your way out of that whole damn scheme."

Margo disappeared through the mudroom door. He next heard the garage door rise, then descend. She was gone.

He looked down at Roberta, who for once did not offer a smile. "Come on, girl."

She traipsed along behind him as he reentered the kitchen and hearth room, where he threw himself against the sofa's cushions. The dog joined him, plopping down at his side. Her master needed comforting.

Ash stared at his phone, then methodically opened his text messages, tapping on the one he hadn't yet seen.

There was the damning statement she'd sent Margo.

Not only is your husband Dr. Ashton Meyers capable of that, but he is complicit in the fraud scheme at Oakwood Specialty Hospital, and know that I've given his name to CMS. Fines and jail time, honey, for your precious husband.

~ ~ ~ ~

Margo restrained herself, controlled her foot on the gas pedal. The last thing she could stand then was to be stopped for speeding or reckless driving. The Doubletree wasn't too far up the road. That location would work just fine until she could get settled, sleep on this – it would require several nights, no doubt – and decide what to do next.

How dare Ash act like it was just an irresistible seduction and one-night stand that he fell for. An unexpected encounter. Right. Two, three days in a row, and God knows how many other trysts. Give me a break. What else had gone on that I failed to detect...was this the only one? What a complete fool she'd been, believing him last Tuesday, trying to take the nuanced, sophisticated approach to a base, crass, all-to-common marital problem. A straying man, who comes crawling back, afraid his good home life has been destroyed. *Too late, buddy. Too late.*

She pulled into the broad drive of the Doubletree and stopped under the porte-cochere. She could conduct all her business from here comfortably, in fact quite comfortably, and wouldn't spare the expense at all. They have a very nice spa, she'd heard.

It was all on his damn dime this time.

And maybe the project in Tulsa needed a bit more hands-on attention, after all.

TWENTY-ONE

Monday

Ash finished the last consult, entering orders in the patient's chart when his cell chimed. He hurriedly slipped it out of his pocket...maybe Margo? His spirit sank. No such luck. It was Kristine Nelson again, requesting he call her. How could he work her in, too? The day had already suffered enough interruptions, and he needed to move on, finish rounds, and stay up with the consults. His week on the hospital duty promised to be a busy one. And his sour mood and emotional exhaustion didn't help.

Scott Feinstein, his attorney and a long-time personal friend, had obliged Ash's early morning call and, once settled at his own office, had rung back. He patiently listened to Ash's diatribe, and agreed the situation presented multiple levels of concern. He asked Ash to come by his office late that afternoon after he'd had time to look into a few things. Maybe they could even grab a bite to eat. Relieved, but time pressured, Ash added that to his list of bases to cover that day. Kristine Nelson might just have to wait.

But she didn't. As the afternoon progressed, he decided to touch base with her. See what she had on her mind. She'd texted no less than three times to summon his attention.

Before he reached the top of the stairs, he saw her head above the receptionist's counter. *My, this woman is anxious. And no assistant in sight.*

She stood abruptly, gave him a tight smile, and gestured toward her office. That afternoon, she was dressed a bit more casually – dress-down Friday on Monday – or the result of an early morning rush? Her black slacks and low-heeled shoes offset a bronze silk blouse and expensive looking matching cardigan, perfectly coordinated with her auburn hair reined in by a suede headband, apparently no time for involved hair designs that morning either. Again minimal jewelry adorned her ear lobes and hands. No sheath, no stilts.

Once inside, she indicated the two chairs fronting her desk, and positioned them facing each other. There would be no large desk barrier between them. Definitely a different comportment and demeanor. Worrisome, or was this perhaps a positive turn?

Ash waited. She held the agenda.

Settled then, and her offer of beverages declined, she said, "Thank you for making time. I know you're very busy today."

He nodded, gave her a half smile.

"It seemed important for us to meet again." She paused and regarded him. "There have been developments in our situation here that have come to my attention."

"Developments?" With him and on his turf for sure…but did this woman know about any of that?

"Yes, developments…significant developments."

"All right…what do you have?"

"Well, last week I became aware of activities on the part of several individuals, which I believe correspond to concerns you expressed two weeks ago."

Translation: she found out staff members or others were up to something. Maybe Erica wasn't so off base after all. He cocked his head and waited. The less he said, the better.

"When you mentioned medical decision-making and

possible staff interference with that."

He nodded. "Yes, those were and are my concerns."

"You see, it is apparently true that several staff have positioned themselves to benefit from full codes on patients, sometimes repeatedly. It's shocking and appalling, really."

"And how might they benefit?"

"In various ways. Basically, it seems…" She cleared her throat, crossed her legs, and draped her forearms over the chair arms, assuming a relaxed posture, then resumed. "So, if they work to keep the patient alive longer, perhaps postponing the inevitable, then our occupancy figures stay strong."

Fully engaged then, Ash pulled her along. "I didn't realize there were occupancy issues here. It always seems full, with patients waiting to get in."

"Well, yes, that is true…most of the time. But…" She shifted in her chair. "There are cycles, you know, to admissions and discharges which create open beds."

"Okay, I understand. So, back to the staff…how do you mean they benefit from full occupancy, specifically?"

Kristine gazed at the bank of windows behind her desk. He glanced over, as well. Was there a problem outside, or was she gathering her thoughts? Apparently, she wrestled with uncomfortable thoughts.

She straightened. "Here's what I know. A few of the staff watch and gather information on patients' DNR status. If someone like Dr. Lange is counseling people to reconsider being a 'no code', then the staff member informs certain other individuals. And their full code status is then re-confirmed."

He'd just have to say it for her; that was obvious. And he didn't have all evening to play verbal games. He was due at Scott Feinstein's office in less than an hour. "Are you getting at a 'heads-in-the-beds' scheme, Kristine?"

She slumped back in her chair rather dramatically, giving him the obvious answer – yes. "It appears so."

"How many of the staff are involved?"

"Less than a dozen, more like half a dozen." She shifted in her chair. "Maybe eight. Yes, about that."

"And what do they receive in return?"

"Better shift scheduling, reimbursement for continuing ed, tuition for advanced degree coursework, incentives like that."

"Who, Kristine, do they report to? Who doles out or ensures these incentives?"

She looked at him directly, her obvious distress out of character. "Dr. Griswold for one, Ric Newman, I believe, but I'm not sure, and...me."

Not altogether shocked by that point, he schooled his expression. "That's quite an admission."

She nodded and looked aside.

"How long has this been going on?"

"Too long." She re-established eye contact, and admitted, "About a year, well, more like six months."

Well, which is it? "So, why are you telling me this now?"

"I need to stop this, and my participation in it."

"Clearly." He paused and waited. Hearing nothing, he asked, "What's your plan?"

"I haven't worked that out in detail. I informed corporate of Dr. Lange's termination, and her activities before that...and some of what she's been up to since."

But hopefully not all she's been up to. "You may have placed her in some danger, Kristine."

She glanced at him, her face stricken. "I realize that now."

"I have a question. You haven't said who exactly provided these benefits to the nurses or other staff. Who, Kristine?" He doubted Todd Griswold would open up his own wallet to pay people. "Or did you reimburse them out of your coffers here?"

"Corporate."

Wow. "Final question...how were the three, or two, of you benefitting from all this?" He already knew the answer, but she needed to say it out loud.

"Bonuses...quarterly bonuses." She crossed and uncrossed her legs, and flicked a tiny piece of lint from her slacks. "And in other ways."

He wasn't going to dig into her last statement. Silence stretched between them. He sat forward and leaned on his elbows. "I'm not sure how confessing all of this to me is going to make any difference. You could work to rectify it without me knowing anything." This was a real turn of affairs, now with this woman going belly up. Wanting his help? He couldn't get any more entangled than he already was.

"You've been interested in Dr. Lange...,"

Whoa, wait a minute.

"and her situation, and I thought we might join forces to resolve this."

"Look, I am not interested in Dr. Lange beyond her telling me she was likely wrongfully terminated. And whether your staff was involved in something akin to fraud. That's your responsibility. And you...you have a very big problem. One I can't resolve for you. I suggest you get legal advice. Quickly. Does Griswold know you're meeting with me?"

"No, no he doesn't."

"Good. Keep it that way." *Where did this bossy tone come from?*

She turned to him directly, scooted forward on her chair. "I want you to know, I'm sincere about getting out of this scheme. Regret is not even a strong enough word for what I feel. I've never done anything like this, ever."

"Well, you have now." Of course, who was he to lecture someone about things they'd never done before?

"Also, I've already had an interview with a different company in another state. It's time to move on."

"It may not be that easy when this whole thing blows open."

"If we work together, don't you think we can keep that from happening, or control the fallout?"

"She's already blown it open, Kristine."

~ ~ ~ ~

Chase stood, cell in hand. "Yes, that's what we need. Exactly." Pause. "As soon as you can; preferably tomorrow."

He listened, impatiently. It was his job to get this done. "Fine, then. Fine."

The party on the other end filled him in on specifics.

"Right. This number for the updates, and you have my email. And don't call my office under any circumstances. Yes. Good." Pause. "Thanks." The short conversation over, the necessary arrangements made, he ended the call.

His day almost done, he turned and gazed out his office windows at the Chicago skyline, the setting sun throwing its last rays through the canyons between buildings. Exhaustion weighed him down. And why would he expect otherwise? He'd spent the past week stressing over the facility in Kansas City spinning out of control. And Kristine Nelson had not handled it. Not well enough. And with what he had on her, well, he could cause that lady and another individual some major grief. So, now it was up to him to re-navigate, alter the course of this initiative. Reconfigure the financial picture, hide information. He shrugged off his fatigue, almost leapt into his desk chair and furiously tapped at his keyboard. He would make the necessary transfers right then; best not wait 'til morning.

And no question they needed to keep an eye on Dr. Lange, and maybe this Dr. Meyers. Was he carrying a torch for her? It'd be easy enough to find out.

TWENTY-TWO

Tuesday

If she didn't call by evening he would contact her, despite her saying she'd be in touch when she chose. They both needed to come to their senses, put this ridiculous situation into perspective, and stay strong together. Granted, he'd screwed up big time and probably needed her more than she needed him, but apart, nothing good would come of this. And Erica Lange, Kristine Nelson, Todd Griswold and any others had no right to drive a wedge between them. Ash coached himself with such thoughts as he shaved and prepared for the day.

The previous day's meeting with Kristine had more than bothered him that night. In one way, it was a relief to know the truth, for her to have come clean. Yes, he was still leery, but leaned toward believing her. Her distress had been palpable. She seemed honest in her stated desire to extricate herself. On the other hand, he now knew too much. How would that shift the equation? Was he back in Erica's court, believing her not-so-wild stories, aiding her whistleblower pursuits? Or, was he at the other end of the court, shooting baskets by himself? After all, she'd effectively thrown him under the bus.

The only thing from Monday which proved encouraging had been sitting down with Scott Feinstein, outlining the whole mess, and the discussion which followed. And the sharing of a beer at a nearby bar after that. Scott efficiently helped organize his thinking, marginalized extraneous thoughts, and coached him to focus his attention on the main points. And quit worrying about which woman to help. His wonderful wife was waiting in the wings, he'd reminded him, and she was the only one worthy of his full attention.

Scott also made it clear he would need to consult with other legals who held credentials in healthcare law, and those with experience with RICO cases. Make use of other opinions, if that's where this was headed. Ash was to get back with him that morning, an assignment he looked forward to. It had been worth every penny Feinstein would charge. Margo was right, again.

There was one other conversation to be had that day, one that would engender lots of questions. And possibly a good deal of stress.

~ ~ ~ ~

Ash pulled into the parking slot a few minutes before noon. He'd achieved a stopping point with rounds at the hospital, and now would beat a path to the attorney's office. Scott was ordering in lunch for them, and they'd finish by one. Nice and neat.

When he approached the large reception desk of Feinstein, Schultz, & Fanning, a comely assistant smiled, rose, and immediately showed him to Scott's office. There was lunch laid out on a side table, two chairs sat at the ready.

They shook hands. "Let's get started," Scott suggested. "So, how was your night?" he asked, as they took their seats, and unwrapped sandwiches and opened bags of chips. Popped open soft drink cans. Good nutrition seemed inconsequential at that moment.

111

"Not real good, to be honest. Our discussion yesterday helped some."

"Heard from Margo?"

"Not yet. I'll call her tonight if she doesn't ring me."

Scott nodded. "I want you to patch it up with her right away, if she'll allow it. You need her as an ally in this, and it's just the right thing to do. She's a fantastic woman, and you're not in a position to be stubborn, Ash."

"Agreed." Tough talk from an attorney and a friend was good. A future divorce consultation, he did not want.

He munched along and listened as Feinstein outlined the plan.

"I've written two letters this morning, and sent them directly to the appropriate people, not just some office. First, to a CMS administrator for this region, Helen Ramsey. I spoke to her earlier and she was expecting my letter. Second, to a top bureaucrat at the state hospital association. I had a good conversation with him before I fired that one off. They both told me that this Dr. Lange had already contacted them. That much we know, but they wouldn't disclose their confidential conversations with her. Of course, we can get that out of them under oath if this progresses." Feinstein frowned for effect and took a swig of soft drink. Ash got the message.

"While you're here, I think we should call this doctor together. And we'll tell her you're here with me. We'll try to assess how put together she is right now. Get her to tell us what else she's done. And I'll encourage her to back off from you in particular, and perhaps shelve her grievances."

"With what Kristine confessed, don't we want Lange's complaint to go forward?"

"Yes, and I don't believe we can stop it now. But whether this Nelson woman plays the role of whistleblower, or Erica does, may make a difference in outcome. Whichever one appears more credible."

"I see your point."

Scott asked, "Do you think Kristine Nelson will assume

that role...with some encouragement?"

"I don't know. I think she just wants to get out of Dodge."

Feinstein leveled a look at Ash. "Tell me again, Ash, were you complicit in this scheme in any way? Did you collude with the facility staff, as Erica maintains?"

Matching the attorney's gaze, Ash said, "Absolutely not, Scott."

"Okay. I just wanted you to confirm that to me again." Taking a swig of his soft drink, he then said, "Let's make that call."

Twenty minutes later, their lunch abandoned, both men wore concerned expressions. Feinstein glanced at his watch. This appointment would be concluded inside of ten minutes. At least they knew where Erica stood – no budging on her part.

"I see what you mean. She's dug in, for sure."

"Look, Scott, I'm concerned for her safety. She has two kids, I told you, two little kids to keep safe. She's the custodial parent. And her ex-husband is off somewhere with his new honey, I think Florida, but still governs whether she can leave this state. He doesn't seem to care about his own kids. I'd like to do something to provide security for her and them."

His attorney studied him. "I'll remind you, Ash, this gal has nearly broken up your marriage, on purpose, and has thrown you under the CMS bus. I'll also remind you that, when CMS comes snooping around about malfeasance and possible fraud, other feds come calling, too. You don't owe her anything. In fact, I'd keep my distance if I were you."

"Can't we arrange for something anonymously?"

Scott stared at him. "You, my friend, are a real softie. Your compassion is admirable, but may be your undoing." After pausing, he admitted, "Yes, we could arrange for a security company to keep an eye on her, and report back to me. But, I caution you, bureaucrats and authorities could easily misinterpret these actions. They don't necessarily understand a *big heart*." He gestured with his hands.

Ash nodded understanding.

After a moment, Feinstein glanced at his watch and said, "I'll look into it."

~ ~ ~ ~

Five o'clock arrived as Ash sat at his desk, shuffling papers, done with the hospital until further consults materialized. His call duties would run for the entire week through the weekend, for their renal patients primarily, and the cardiologist's over the weekend. That colleague had scheduled an out-of-town commitment with his grown kids. The cross coverage, and give and take, suited everyone, but this week Ash wished he had less to do.

The group's managing partner Dr. Mitchell Burns was in the office all week and would soon be done seeing his scheduled pulmonary patients. The office was settling down and shortly the staff would depart. Perhaps he could broach the subject without staff eavesdropping, and without having to wait until their next official group meeting. The group needed to address this issue. But his partner needed to be informed and prepared ahead of time. He sent him a simple text.

Twenty minutes later, Burns stuck his head in the door. "Still have some time?"

"Sure. I was waiting on you."

Entering, the other physician took a side chair. "How's Margo? The boys?"

"Good, good."

"How's her design business going? I think Judy may call her about a project."

"Going well. She's busy right now with a commercial client in Tulsa, but she'll be back soon." *I hope.* "Have Judy give her office a call, and I'll give Margo a heads up." *If I ever reach her.*

His colleague settled in, Ash leaned back in his chair and tried to relax. "There's an issue at Specialty which I think the group needs to address."

His friend eyed him. "Oh, what sort of issue? A problem?"

"Yes, I'd call it a problem." Burns waited. Ash continued, "Apparently, Todd Griswold let Dr. Lange go a couple of weeks back."

"The brunette beauty? I hadn't heard that."

"Right. So, they were unhappy with her counseling patients about end-of-life procedures, in particular DNR status. Seems they felt she pressured everyone there to declare themselves DNR."

"I wasn't aware."

"Me, either. Until Friday, October eleventh." *How will I ever forget that date?* "Anyway, she didn't take that very well, and decided she was wrongfully terminated. But what she found out after that is the big deal."

His partner gave him a frown, which transformed into a questioning look.

"At first I didn't believe her. It seems a number of staff made note of her conversations and reported back to higher ups. And they were rewarded for doing so."

"Whew…"

"Yeah. Anyway, she had other staff who fed her information as well, about how certain nurses were reimbursed for their cooperation."

"So, how did you get involved?"

"She told me about it earlier this month, and then again the following week." *Boy, did she.*

"At first when I heard this, she said we had to get the social workers' or DON's okay to change someone's status. Said it was considered discharge planning. That they had to agree with it, or we couldn't counsel patients and families without them being present and agreeing with the change. I voiced my objections to the COO Kristine Nelson on two occasions about our autonomous medical decision-making. And that other personnel could not interfere with our role, unless it was a very unusual circumstance."

"Well, I would agree with that."

"I even obtained the facility's written policy from Kristine. There's no such rule. Then she said she would have their lawyers take a look again at the document's wording. All that changed when Kristine Nelson spoke with me yesterday. I'm telling you this in confidence right now, because I believe we may need to consider withdrawing from our position there."

"Withdraw?" Burns shifted in his chair. "Go on."

"She, Kristine that is, confessed that she and Griswold were receiving quarterly bonuses for keeping people alive. Maybe Ric Newman, too. Heads-in-the-beds sort of thing."

"What?" Looking stunned, his partner straightened.

"Right. She expressed remorse, says she wants out of there, and is moving on."

"Doesn't she know that won't make her problem go away? They'll find her if they want to." Burns paused, then asked, "Why do you think she told you this?"

"Kristine believes I know everything about Erica's situation and allegations, and she regrets her own involvement. And she implied during our first discussion, that we – our group – set patients and families up for unrealistic expectations during their hospitalizations, and bear some responsibility for creating this situation in the first place, before they're transferred to Specialty. Plain and simple, she wants me on her team now, to help protect her."

"You aren't, are you?"

"No way. But I do know some of what Erica plans to do. To start with, she's already contacted the CMS regional office and the state hospital association. She's hell bent on filing a wrongful termination suit against Griswold and his internal medicine group."

"Does Kristine know all this?"

"I haven't told her what Erica's confided in me, no. But,

there may be other ways she's found out. She didn't say. I bet she's worried, though, about who knows what. And about corporate's response. She said they paid the bonuses and authorized her, Griswold, and others to take care of the staff, in turn."

"Man, sounds like a mess."

"Right." The two men sat in silence for what seemed a long time.

Burns spoke next. "Look, it's getting late. Let me mull this over. We won't go forward and discuss this with the group yet. I'm on over there next week and can observe now with eyes wide open. See if I pick up on anything." He studied his hands. "When's Kristine leaving?"

"She didn't say. But she's already interviewed with a different company in another state. I do know that much."

"Does anyone else know about this?"

"Well, apparently all the various players, but no one else here." *And Margo, who's out running around somewhere, madder than hell.* "I've consulted my personal attorney. It seemed prudent."

His colleague nodded, rose, and stood in place. "Man." He turned toward the door, then pivoted. "I'm glad you told me. But I don't relish the rough ride we may be in for. Let me know what your lawyer says. We need to stay in touch." With that he exited and made his way toward the back entrance.

Rough ride, to say the least. And he hadn't even told Burns the 'brunette beauty' had already thrown him, G. Ashton Meyers, under the bus.

~ ~ ~ ~

They watched as he left the building and strode toward his SUV, his head bowed. It was obvious from his picture they'd pulled up on their screens that it was Dr. Grant Ashton Meyers. He wasn't hard to pick out from a crowd. His tall stature and all-American-boy good looks certainly helped distinguish him. He was alone, as expected.

Sitting in their truck, one row away from Ash's vehicle and facing his building, they enjoyed a clear view of him as he emerged. But, they doubted he'd pay a moment's attention to the two of them, outfitted in ball caps and shades, old jackets and jeans, sporting several days' growth of beard. One middle-age, one much younger, busy with their devices, as if waiting on a family member to rejoin them after an appointment somewhere in the medical office building. Not a notable sight at all.

They watched as he slid into the driver's seat of his car, and sat for a few moments. It appeared he was fiddling with his phone, but they couldn't tell for sure. Exchanging a look, the younger man got out, and moved to the hood of their truck, while the older man pulled the hood release latch. Feigning concern for some malfunctioning component under the hood, the younger man glanced around, acted as if he had just spotted Ash, and ambled toward his SUV. He stood apart until he caught Ash's attention. The doctor rolled down his window.

"Yeah?"

He felt Ash's eyes rake over him, sizing him up. "Hey, we got a problem over here with our truck. Won't start. Battery, probly."

Ash glanced back to where the young man gestured. "Okay."

"You got some cables?"

"I do. Which truck is yours?"

"The black one there." He gestured in the general direction of the truck. His comrade raised his hand in a friendly two-finger salute.

"Sure."

Ash rolled up his window, and maneuvered his vehicle to position in front of the beat-up, dirty truck. The driver gave him a broad smile. He jumped out, retrieved his cables from the SUV's rear compartment, and joined the younger man under the truck's hood. He looked up, gave the driver the signal to start the engine. No click. Ash motioned them to stop.

"It doesn't act like your battery." He bent over, inspected a few things before he noticed the loose distributor cap. He quickly straightened, and shot the younger man a look. Picking up the laid-aside jumper cables, it was clear the doctor was on guard.

The young man smiled. "Gee...I guess you're right. How'd that happen? This crappy old thing...wouldn't surprise me anything could've gone wrong."

Ash stepped back, smiled and said, "Glad it was that simple. You can take care of it, I'm sure."

"You bet."

The men watched as Ash wasted no time striding to his vehicle, and gripping the SUV door handle, said, "You fellas have a good evening."

The two observed him pull away slowly, while keeping one eye on his side-view mirror. He was suspicious for sure. They then spotted their female companion, dressed in sloppy sweats, her old car coat flapping in the breeze, emerge from the office building and hurry towards their truck. Great! Her appearance ought to mask their ruse, and reassure the good doctor – if he's looking – that they were for real.

Their woman jumped into the back seat. The driver put the truck in gear and watched as Ash accelerated and made his way to the parking lot exit.

Their assessment: he was a real nice guy, good looking, too, a straight arrow, and would help anyone in need.

And he was no fool.

TWENTY-THREE

Wednesday

She only needed to plan for two, three days max. A carryon would suffice. Laundry done, Erica stood and stared at her clothing choices spread out on the bed. She needed to select fairly conservative interchangeable outfits, nothing too trendy, and nothing sexy. This was a business matter, and she needed to look the part. She picked up and put down several turtleneck sweaters, a couple of silk blouses, and two pairs of slacks. Several versatile jackets. Layering one on top of the other, she mixed and matched until she was pleased with her selections. And sensible shoes, two pairs – one for travel, one to change into for her meeting. No stilts. She needed to be fleet of foot.

Jewelry choices were easy – minimal, conservative, no big rocks. Gazing in the mirror then, she assessed her mane of black hair. She messed around with various arrangements until one struck her as becoming, but conservative. Tied up in a twist she looked like business, but a woman who could be talked into pleasure, though not too easily. Perfect. She packed several hair combs to achieve the intended look. Now to her toiletries and she'd be done.

She chose a light fragrance this time, pleasant floral notes, but nothing heavy, nothing seductive. She wouldn't detract from her appearance with a perfume which sent the wrong message. It was all in the packaging.

That done, she turned to the stacks of folded laundry and made her way to the kids' rooms. She needed to get their things ready, too, including their costumes. At Riley's door, she stopped abruptly. What was she doing to these little ones? Halloween at their Aunt Susan's, their mother off on a trip? Why couldn't she have waited just another week? She knew why.

~ ~ ~ ~

Out in the street, and around the bend from her sprawling ranch, sat two men waiting for some action. She hadn't emerged again after running the kids to school before eight that morning. Now, they were hunkered down for the day with food and supplies, wishing for something notable to happen. The neighbors might wonder, and wander over. Still, they had an assignment and would need to report to Agent Cline by day's end, whether it proved to be exciting or nothing.

She didn't appear to keep an animal so wouldn't come outside to service a pet. They hoped she ran or rode a bike for exercise. That, at least, would be something. And eventually, she would need to pick up her kids again, unless they rode the bus home that day. Sometimes they did, while other times she collected them herself. That much they also knew.

One kept watch, the other tended to his device. The garage door suddenly rose, and Erica emerged with a full trash bag in hand. Both took notice. She wore yoga pants, a loose long-sleeved yellow T-shirt, and some sort of athletic shoes. She walked straight to a large trash bin already at her curb, deposited the bag, and stared down the street. Perhaps she'd go for a jog? No such luck.

A few moments later, she returned to her garage, the

door slid down, and she disappeared from sight. It didn't appear to them she thought anything of their lawn care company truck, with its colorful logo emblazoned on the side panels, sitting there along the curb, pointing toward her home. Best though to drive through the nearby streets and reposition the vehicle.

If she left in the meantime, or made any calls, they'd know about it. Thank goodness for all their high-tech monitoring tools. And the plumber would arrive in about twenty minutes. His claim: there was a notice of a clogged main sewer line he needed to attend to on her lot. Question was, would she give him the time of day, maybe come outside and interact?

Rounding the corner on their three-block target area, and approaching her house from the opposite direction, they noted a black, rather rough-looking truck slow down as it passed her property. Who were those guys? Had Cline sent another team? Passenger agent quickly texted as they passed by, noting two men in the front seat. He received a response almost immediately – 'no, to an extra team, and what do you have so far'? Their answer: 'Nothing noteworthy about her. A black truck cruising by. Seems interested, too.'

It was time to get out somewhere along the street and perform lawn care. Now there were two parties to keep an eye on. This had become interesting, after all. There was that house two doors down where both adults had left for work that morning. They'd start there and clip a few bushes. No one would think a thing of it.

Forty-five minutes later, and done with their limited trimming, the two looked up when Erica's garage door rose. She punched in the door code, sending it down again. Putting their tools away in their truck they pretended to ignore her movements. She checked something attached to her waistband, then took off jogging in the opposite direction. Perfect...they could circle around and keep track of her course.

~ ~ ~ ~

Erica, lost in thought, rounded the curve approximately a quarter mile from her home just as the landscape company van circled by. Both men waved or nodded, acknowledging their observation of her. Not an unusual experience at all when she passed workmen of any sort. She'd grown immune to their various greetings. Best to ignore that type, anyway. Listening to a podcast, she caught a glimpse in her peripheral vision of someone waving. She turned and saw a neighbor smiling at her. The woman jogged toward her on the sidewalk. Erica pulled up and stopped, glad for a brief rest. She hadn't gotten in as many days of exercise as typical for her due to her recent schedule. And was feeling rather out of shape. Which was not an excuse, really.

She removed her earbuds. "Hi, Becca."

"Hey there."

"How've you been?"

"Not bad. I won't keep you, but..." Just as she spoke, the 'lawn boys' drove past, pretending to check for other addresses. Becca threw them a sharp eye, then looked away. She spoke to Erica in a conspiratorial tone, "There they are again."

Erica cast a glance in their direction, but they'd disappeared down the street. "Who?"

"That van with the two guys in it. Didn't you see them earlier?"

"Guess I didn't pay any attention. I did see a couple of guys trimming bushes about two doors down this morning."

"Well, that's them and there's another truck cruising around. They've been by three times that I've noticed."

Erica glanced about. "That kitchen window of yours works pretty well, doesn't it?" Realizing she conveyed a smart aleck tone, she grew serious. "Not a delivery truck?" she clarified.

"Heavens, no. It was black, seen better days, with two rough-looking guys in it. You should be careful out here running by yourself."

"I'm sure it's nothing. But I'm careful, and take precautions. Say, while I've got you...could you make sure my trash can gets back up by the garage this Friday?"

"Sure. I can put it away. Going out of town?"

"Yeah, I have a trip to Chicago tonight. I'll only be gone a couple of days."

"Where are the kids staying?"

"With my sister."

"No problem. I'll take care of it."

"I'll give you the garage code before I leave, if you'll be here later."

"All afternoon. You be careful now. Keep an eye out." Her neighbor glanced in both directions again, gave her some sort of hand signal, then retreated up her driveway, dragging a wide-ranging hose behind her.

"Always," Erica reassured her. With a wave, she resumed jogging. She repositioned her shades, left out her earbuds, and prepared to better monitor her surroundings.

As annoying as Becca's interest was in everyone's business up and down the street, she still took the woman's observations seriously. Sometimes the best security was a nosy neighbor. Never a bad idea to be alert and aware, and heed such warnings. Not with what was going on.

~ ~ ~ ~

In his study, Ash observed the eastern horizon as the sun set behind him. He marveled at the hues of the rarefied vista. Intense blues fading into purples in the evening sky, dotted with mounded coral thunderheads. But that evening the view brought little solace.

Three rings, four rings...was she going to pick up? Or, was she out with the charming client in Tulsa? He didn't even know for sure where she'd gone. Five rings and the voice message greeting spoke. He would not leave some inane comment. He didn't need to; she knew who was calling. Ash clicked off.

The previous evening he'd also failed to reach her. Or, she'd failed to respond. Straining to control his irritation, he turned his attention to emails which had piled up over the past two days. He really couldn't blame Margo for any of this, and his irritation with her was unfounded. But still...

His cell chimed. Her face appeared on the caller ID. He waited until two rings had elapsed, then answered. "Hi there."

"You called. Has something happened with the boys?"

"I did." Silence intervened. Were they going to strain to manufacture a conversation? "No, nothing with the boys. I just wanted to make sure you're okay, and that things are going well for you."

"Things going well? That's a strange thing to say, don't you think, given the circumstances."

"Maybe."

After a pause, she said, "Things are as expected. I wouldn't call this okay, but it's going along. You?"

"I don't know where to start. Some things have shifted." Margo said nothing, and he went on, "I spoke with Scott Feinstein Monday and again yesterday. He's helping. You were right."

"That's good...that he's helping."

"He and I called Dr. Lange yesterday while I was at his office. She's fixed on her plan, won't be deterred."

"Why doesn't that surprise me?"

"Right. Well, he's written several letters already to a couple of agencies, and he's developed a strategy to deal with her and the situation at Oakwood Specialty."

"So, am I supposed to feel reassured about that?"

"No, and I'm not either, yet. But something good and appropriate has been initiated."

"There is nothing good and appropriate about the situation, Ash, not at all."

"Right again." He paused. Not unexpectedly, nothing he said was sufficient. The silence hung heavy between them.

He sucked in a big breath and said, "Margo, look, I didn't call to make you angry. I fucked up royally, and I know it. But, you need to know those pictures she sent were a set-up. She fabricated that incident." No comment came forth. Ash went on, "You know I love you, always have, and I need you. Our relationship, our marriage is more important than any of this, and I want to repair the damage I've done. I don't hold you responsible for any of this." He huffed out his pent-up breath. "I don't fault you for being furious. And I don't expect you to plaster on a smile and come running back just because I've said these things."

"I won't."

His stomach clenched. Had he lost this woman altogether? Suddenly exhaustion, a heavy weight, fell on his shoulders. "I just wanted to hear your voice, Margo."

~ ~ ~ ~

She glanced at the large monitor suspended on the wall. The concourse in the American terminal was moderately busy for a Wednesday evening. She found her flight number, confirmed the gate hadn't changed, and noted it was listed as 'on time'. It was a considerable walk around the KCI terminal before reaching the security portal for her gate. A good walk before her flight. Erica took off at a fair clip.

Everything was going as planned.

~ ~ ~ ~

He spotted her striding toward him down the concourse. Not your average looking woman, she was easy to keep an eye on. Dressed in his long-sleeve blue button down, khaki slacks, casual loafers, and sport coat resting in his lap, he appeared as any business traveler might, departing for an out-of-town meeting. Fiddling with his cell phone, earbuds in place. This being his usual attire when he worked as an Air Marshall, or as in this case, when he performed this function for the Bureau. Yes, she was very easy to keep track of. He watched several heads turn as she passed by. He'd wait a bit, then follow along to the gate. Certainly not unpleasant to sit by such a beautiful woman, with one seat open between them. And no one would occupy that middle seat, not on that flight, they had made sure. He'd have all the time he needed to chat her up. This might be a fun little assignment, after all.

Unless the business in Chicago went south.

TWENTY-FOUR

October 31st

Thursday

The elevator rose silently and swiftly through the shaft to the twentieth floor. Three fit-appearing electricians – garbed in navy blue jumpsuits, clean yellow t-shirts peeking through at their open collars, and matching running shoes – exited at that floor, gloves and tool chests in hand. Two had forgotten to get haircuts for a month, the other had forgotten to shave that morning. If they looked too groomed, their true career choice might have been suspected. The logo emblazoned above their chest pockets, and on the side of the cases they carried, let everyone know they were from Windy City Electrical.

No such service call had been requested by the business. Windy City had reportedly been summoned by the building's manager to make routine maintenance assessments of the electrical infrastructure in preparation for enhancements needed by 5G networks. None of which was true or necessary, but they were certain no receptionist or office manager would question the veracity of their appearance. To back them up, they were equipped with a written work order in triplicate, of course, to support that summons, which bore the building manager's forged signature, no less.

They glanced in both directions, and headed to the glass double doors at the end of the hall, the most experienced of the trio in the lead. Once admitted to the interior, they would spread out, cover all of the three main halls in the suite and commence their work.

The striking young blond receptionist – resembling more a Swedish model than serious receptionist – looked up as they entered, her face registering surprise.

"Windy City Electrical," the lead man informed her with a smile.

She stood, returned his friendly expression, and visually assessed the three men, not an unpleasant job for a young unattached woman.

"One moment," she said, sinking back down and examining the day's schedule on her computer screen.

One of the younger men leaned casually on the tall countertop, making sure he smiled every time she looked up or made eye contact. Useful preliminaries if she was prone to check with the building super about such mundane matters as work orders. After clicking around, she looked up and let them know, "I don't see any work scheduled for today. We haven't received a notice."

"Correct," the lead man replied. Taking charge, he placed both hands, palms down, on the polished granite countertop. "The order came in early this morning. Said it was important. You've just not received notice of it, yet."

The young leaning man caught her eye, smiled, and winked.

Disarmed, she looked at all three men. "I'm sure you're right. I didn't catch your names."

The lead man motioned to himself. "I'm Chad. This is Thad and that's Brad." They'd practiced enough so as to maintain straight faces throughout the introduction, save smiling at her.

Apparently not questioning such a series of obvious bogus names, she then asked, "And I'm Christy. Where are you supposed to start?"

Gesturing toward an interior wood-framed glass door, Chad said, "In the three main halls, Christy."

One of his colleagues consulted the work order secured on a metal box clipboard. He affirmed, "That's what it says here."

"Won't you come this way?" she invited, leading them toward the interior door.

They followed, enjoying the view as she led them to the inner sanctum. Once through the doors, they thanked her profusely, the lead man directing his subordinates to the respective interior halls.

They busied themselves setting up, laid out tools and other paraphernalia to perform their job, but not the job outlined on the fake work order. They also kept an eye on her until she returned to the reception foyer. Once she was gone, they ambled through the halls, pretending to inspect wall outlets, removing a few covers. Along the way, they checked out the private office occupancies up and down each hall. About thirty percent occupied that day, no group meetings underway. In fact, they noted the large conference room sat empty, waiting for what might happen next. This was not going to be difficult, after all, but one never knew for sure going in. They had about fifteen or twenty minutes until the others would arrive.

~ ~ ~ ~

Erica gazed out the windows as the cab sped along the highway. It was cloudy, the well-defined low gray ceiling hung barely above the tall buildings, and the temperature chilly, but not considered cold for October in the Midwest. They skirted the downtown area and would soon dive into the corridors of Chicago business. It wouldn't take long before she would arrive.

Admittedly, she was tired from lack of sleep the night before. It neared midnight by the time she had reached her hotel, and sleep did not come soon. Still, she'd awakened early and felt energized to get on with the day. Now, though, her hyped-up energy reserve lagged. Her stomach, too empty, felt queasy. A pang for her children unsettled her. Her plan, once launched, hopefully wouldn't take long to execute, and she could get back home right away. Time to move on.

~ ~ ~ ~

"I'm telling you, Ash, she left town last night. Flew out of KCI around eight. Our woman followed her there, parked and went inside, saw her go through security at a set of gates. Only two in that section had scheduled flights last night. She either went to Chicago or Las Vegas. We suspect the former since the corporate headquarters are there."

Ash sat in the small doctor's dictation room and listened to Feinstein without interrupting. The attorney had not actually told him whether they'd set up security on Erica Lange or not. Now, it was obvious they had. He glanced around for eavesdroppers, waited, then said, "So, what has the security detail observed otherwise?"

"Not a lot. Pretty routine stuff. They suspect at least one other party is tailing her, probably since early this week. And another small group cruises around frequently in a used-looking truck."

Ash sat forward in his chair. "Used truck?"

"Yeah, that's what they reported. And only because they noticed it several times. Seemed out of place in her neighborhood."

"What color truck?"

"Black."

"My God." Pressure building in his head, he couldn't speak for several moments.

He heard Feinstein's voice, seemingly in the distance. "Something wrong, Ash?"

When he opened his mouth, nothing came out. Forcing his words then, he squeaked, "May…" He cleared his throat and continued, "May be the same bunch who asked me for help in the parking lot."

"What are you talking about?"

"Tuesday…when I left my office, two guys sitting in an older, dirty black truck asked me for help. There wasn't anything wrong. They were faking it, had loosened their distributor cap. I got out of there, but saw a woman come out of my building and climb in, acting like she'd come from a medical appointment. Pretty good ruse. They sure looked the part."

"Why didn't you let me know this?"

"I don't know. I put it aside. Was intent on talking with Margo that night. Yesterday was god-awful busy."

Feinstein let out a heavy sigh. "Right." Silence stretched. "So, did you reach Margo?"

"Yeah, last night."

"And how'd it go?"

"So, so. I did most of the talking."

"Not a good sign, usually."

"Right. Anyway, back to the doctor and her travels. What's your opinion?"

"That she took off for Chicago and the headquarters. Storm the place, stir things up. Who knows."

"And we don't have someone on her?"

"No. We don't, but apparently at least one other group does. And my guess is the agencies she's talked to. Probably CMS. And if there's a claim of fraud, they muster other groups."

"Other groups?"

"The FBI…I'll remind you."

TWENTY-FIVE

The cab pulled to the curb, stopped abruptly, and the driver recited the amount. She slid her card through the reader, added a tip, and completed her transaction. Her heart beat hard. She was finally there, and suddenly not sure her plan represented sound reasoning on her part. Perhaps any wisdom she'd ever accumulated had flown. But, truthfully, that had already occurred several weeks ago. The driver handed her a small paper receipt, she climbed out of his vehicle, and off he sped.

Left alone on the sidewalk, save passersby, Erica glanced up and down the street at the towering buildings blocking the view. She strode toward the large glass entry doors. This was it, the completion of her efforts.

~ ~ ~ ~

Chase Monroe stood in his office door and watched the electrician working in the hall. No one had said anything about maintenance that day. All the lights were still on, and his computer hummed along, so obviously they hadn't shut off the power yet.

133

Taking a few steps into the hall, he approached the young man. "What's the issue?"

A friendly face returned his inquiry. "Just routine work, sir, throughout the building."

Chase stuck out his hand, "Chase Monroe."

The young man stood, and the two men shook hands. The electrician, pointing to his embroidered name badge, said, "Thad."

"How long will this take, Thad?"

"Not sure. We'll see."

"Will you let us know if you have to interrupt the power so we can save our files, and turn off our computers appropriately?"

Thad smiled. "Sure. No worries."

Chase retreated into his office. No email had hit his inbox about planned electrical maintenance. There were important documents to review that morning, and a power interruption or failure could screw things up. Back at his desk then, he attacked his keyboard with renewed gusto, skipping around, saving files here and there just in case. He pulled a couple of jump drives from a drawer and got busy. He didn't want the work he'd already done to vanish, even temporarily.

~ ~ ~ ~

At the front desk, the receptionist glanced up as Erica came through the doors, less than ten minutes later. The name plate informed her Christy was on duty.

Prior to making her way to the twentieth floor, she'd scoped out the lobby, feigning a search at the interior marquee for the office she sought. There did not appear to be individuals who resembled agents of the government loitering about, although two younger men in business casual scoped her out. They could be something to watch, but she chose at that moment to ignore their interest. Admittedly, since her cautious neighbor's nosiness the day before, she'd been uneasy and on alert. You never knew who might be following you around, and they can certainly create clever disguises.

After a time, a security guard had approached and inquired whether she would require any assistance, which she declined. She then made her way to the ladies' room to refresh her appearance. Looking her best was requisite to success. She had always known her looks disarmed others, and she intended to put it to good use that day. Hair flying around, smudged mascara, or clothes out of kilter would not cut it. She'd adjusted her blouse and jacket, smoothed her skirt, and made sure the edge of her bra wasn't digging and rubbing. Being reasonably comfortable was a good idea, too. After her preparations, she left the restroom and moved toward the elevator, only a short wait for an empty car followed.

"Hello, how may I assist you?" Christy asked in pleasant tone.

"I am here to see Mr. Monroe, please."

She felt Christy's eyes scraping over her, at least to the extent she could assess her from the chest up.

"One moment." Christy consulted her computer screen, likely looking for excuses to deny her request. "And you are?"

"Kristine Nelson, Oakwood Specialty, Kansas City."

She was out on a limb here, not knowing for sure whether Ms. Nelson had ever met with Chase Monroe in person. And of course he could look her up instantaneously. Still, an off-guard surprise moment might work in her favor.

"One moment, please. Would you like to have a seat?"

"I'm more comfortable standing, but thank you." She'd need to move forward as soon as Chase came through the door, if he did, so as to catch him in the moment. He would hopefully avoid making a scene in front of the lovely Christy. Or her appearance at his office door would do the trick.

Christy spoke in low tones to her phone intercom system, looked up, and smiled. Erica feigned interest in the assorted artwork gracing the walls of the reception foyer.

They appeared to be real oil paintings – large, colorful landscapes invoking peaceful scenes, giving off warm vibes. Well-done, and expensive.

A few moments later, Christy rose and gestured to Erica. "Won't you come this way?" she said, moving toward the interior doors.

Without responding, Erica fell in behind her, relieved that recognition and confrontation would come in the private hall or once she was in his office. Perhaps, though, he didn't know at all what Kristine Nelson looked like. What an interesting twist that could be.

As they entered a particular hall, Christy turned slightly and informed her, "It's busy around here this morning with all this electrical work going on."

Erica noted a nice-looking young man crouched near a wall, working diligently as she and Christy approached Chase Monroe's door. He looked up, swiftly checked her out, and nodded. Her neck tingled as they passed. There was something about his visual assessment which seemed odd, a bit too thorough, a bit too deliberate.

They arrived at the door which stood partially open. She could see well enough the large space she was about to enter. A bank of windows flanked the opposite wall. Christy stood aside, pushing open the door. "Mr. Monroe, this is Kristine Nelson."

He stood and smiled. No recognition or question lit his face. Her first thought – *Chase Monroe has never met Kristine Nelson in person, or he is terrifically skilled at controlled expression.*

"Do come in, Ms. Nelson."

Perhaps he is about to drop the façade once the blond leaves. Erica returned his smile, entered the office, and remained standing.

Christy closed the door behind them. At last.

He stepped forward, extending his hand. "Chase Monroe. I don't believe we've actually met before."

"No, no we haven't, Mr. Monroe." She was not going to

restate her name at that moment; that would come soon enough.

"Please have a seat. And it's Chase." He gestured toward two upholstered side chairs, which coordinated with the carpet, grass-cloth wall coverings, and several paintings gracing the walls. Retractable window shades hung at half-mast, despite no sun to block. Certainly, a sanctuary where he could execute his business.

"Thank you."

He reclined in his desk chair and studied her. Had he just realized his mistake? Granted she and Kristine were both the same height, and their hair might seem similar in dark lighting. And with her own swept up for this encounter, it might be mistaken for the auburn tresses of her assumed character. But the resemblance stopped there. They'd never be mistaken for each other. Erica reined in her analysis and returned his regard.

Finally, he spoke, his tone a bit firm. "It's rather amazing you came all that way to pop in like this. Is there a specific reason for your visit? I would have thought you'd schedule ahead."

"Yes, well, I felt it was necessary to come in person to discuss our arrangement. And the trip developed rather spur of the moment."

"Our arrangement." It was not a question. "What in particular needs further discussion now?"

He's stalling for time. "The issue of Dr. Erica Lange and her untimely departure. It seems she's moving toward a wrongful termination suit. And there's more."

He steepled his fingers, and stared at her. "More?"

"Yes, Chase, more. I believe the bonus plan is unraveling."

"How so? If my memory serves me, you covered that last Thursday."

Uh-oh, small oversight. They've talked. "There are others who know of it, thanks to Dr. Lange. Others at the facility, in the community, and at federal agencies."

137

That got his attention. He snapped forward in his seat, leaned his forearms on the desk. A dark look crept over his face. "How did you come to know this?"

"Through those close to the situation, and my own discussions with CMS personnel."

"Why didn't you inform me of this before now, especially if you've had discussion with anyone at CMS? Did they call you?"

"No, Chase, I called them." Her stomach clenched. The moment was at hand. Feeling strangely dizzy, she held on for his next question.

"What? Why would you do such a thing?"

"Because, Chase…" She stood, suddenly wobbly as she said his name, "I am Dr. Erica Lange."

TWENTY-SIX

Not able to conceal his shock, his eyes narrowed, as if trying to bring her face into better focus. Slowly he got to his feet. "So, you're the one."

"Yes, I'm the one."

Hands on his hips, he stood in place behind his desk. Within minutes a creeping smile spread his lips and softened his hard chin.

Erica said nothing and refrained from returning his smile. This man was cunning, and she'd best remain on alert, ready to move. But dizziness controlled her, the pit in her stomach gnawed.

A noise from the hall broke the silent tension. At once, behind Erica, the office door opened, and an electrician stuck his head in. A furious Chase glared at the intruder. "What?"

"Excuse me, sir, but I need to get in here to check some electrical connections."

"Can't this wait?"

What is happening?

"Afraid not, sir."

"Well, make it quick, then. The lady and I will find another place." Chase closed out his computer screen and rounded his desk.

Where is he about to take me?

He closed the short distance between them. His hand cupping her elbow, he ushered her toward the door. As the electrician stepped aside, two suited men suddenly materialized. Chase dropped his support of her elbow. No more pseudo-gallantry.

Erica braced an arm against the nearby wall, stared at the newcomers – the official-looking newcomers – and froze in place.

"Please step aside, Dr. Lange," one instructed her.

Unable to move, she wasn't sure who to obey. *Who are these men messing up my plan? How do they know who I am?*

Firmly then, one repeated, "Step aside, ma'am."

She did as instructed, taking up residence behind one of the upholstered chairs, gripping its top edge for support, and staring as the electrician – now a reincarnated federal agent – entered the office and went straight to Chase Monroe's desk.

Chase protested, "Hey, you can't do that. Leave my computer alone. What gives you the right?"

One of the agents, the more senior of the trio, reached into his jacket pocket, produced a leather packet, and flipped it open for all to see. "This gives him the right to do that, Mr. Monroe. Special Agent in Charge, Robert Cline."

Chase stared, wide-eyed at the cred pack, and muttered choice expletives for all to hear.

"Proceed, Agent Thane." The young agent commenced working the computer, removing all manner of hardware for their examination.

As she remained fixed in place, Erica became aware of notable noise. Movement noises. Firm voices issuing orders, some other muted angry voices. The entire office suite had come alive.

Christy charged down the hall in one direction, then flew by again within minutes, likely trying to find an escape route. *No way out but the front door, honey.* How many people here were in on this thing? Likely only a few key players, but those few would sink the whole lot of them. And what would be her own next move?

She didn't have to wait long for an answer.

"Come this way, ma'am," Agent Cline instructed. He motioned to her, clearly ordering her to leave the office with him.

A wave of nausea and lightheadedness swept over her. She stopped in the doorway, gripped the door frame, and lowered her head. Granted she hadn't eaten much of anything that morning, but this was different. "Are you all right, Doctor?"

"No, I'm not. I must sit down."

"Can you make it to the conference room?"

He obviously didn't want her back in Chase Monroe's office with the computer confiscation underway. She certainly agreed with that idea. And she wanted to get as far away from Chase as she could manage.

She glanced up and nodded. "We'll see. I can try. May have to stop in route."

"You give the signal."

He cupped her elbow and, at a fair clip, ushered her down the hall and around the corner. Her vision partially recovered, and putting one foot in front of the other, she focused on making it to the protection of a more private enclosure.

As they neared the conference room door, she saw a woman waiting at the table. A full-figured mature woman, who wore a no-nonsense expression. Who on earth was this? Another agent with the Bureau? Her answer came momentarily.

Obviously reading the situation correctly, the woman's expression transformed to one of concern. Cline spoke, "This is Dr. Lange. She's not feeling well." He assisted Erica to the closest chair, deposited her there, and finished introductions. "Doctor, this is Helen Ramsey."

Erica, lightheaded and overwhelmed again by nausea, stared at the woman across from her. At that moment, pain shot through her lower abdomen and, gripping her midsection, she lowered her head to the table. It didn't matter who this was.

"What on earth?" Helen exclaimed, immediately leaving her chair and coming to Erica's side. "Honey, what is wrong?"

Erica lolled her head from side to side, hoping that sufficed for 'I don't know'. She suddenly felt a warmth between her legs. *Could it be?*

Cline, looking askance, stood nearby. "Should we call someone?"

Helen knelt beside Erica's chair and said, "I think we must. Please do that."

Cline stepped out to summon the paramedics.

Helen readdressed Erica, "We should lay you down. Here let me help."

"I'm...I think I'm bleeding," she managed to inform Helen. She had to get flat, but pain paralyzed her. This woman, this CMS bureaucrat, was her only help?

"Bleeding?" As she peeled Erica from the chair and rolled her to the floor, she uttered, "Oh, my yes." Then recognition lit her face. "Oh, hon..."

Erica struggled to focus on Helen, and admitted, "May be pregnant."

She felt Helen's warm hand grip hers.

"Hang on, hon. Help's coming."

In the distance, she heard Cline's voice and other noises, and finally Helen saying, "Oh, God."

The tight band around her left arm hurt. She roused. Someone held her other arm, and a sharp prick caused her to recoil. *Who's attacking me?*

"Hold still, Doctor. We're starting an IV."

"Blood pressure's ninety over sixty, pulse one-ten," she heard the other paramedic say.

Erica opened her eyes and managed to raise her head slightly, saw a man and a woman beside her, and Helen's face near her feet. What had happened? Had she passed out? A chill ran through her. Shivering she couldn't control overtook her. She rolled her head from side to side. Could she clear the cobwebs, clear her thinking?

"What's matter?" she managed. She felt cold running up her left arm. Someone was touching her right thigh. What were they doing? Examining her? She reached down, despite the tight cuff around her right arm, felt for her clothes. They were all askew. She worked to push them back down.

"Good...you're coming around."

"Coming where?"

Someone laid a hand on her forehead, and said, "Look at me."

It was the woman at her side. Erica strained to focus on that person.

"We're the paramedics. We'll get things stabilized then take you to the hospital."

"Hospital," she repeated. Fragments of scenes poked through – Chase Monroe's face, big paintings, men in suits, hurrying down the hall – all coming into sharper focus.

"Yes, the hospital. Looks like you're miscarrying. Did you know you were pregnant?"

"She's had about five hundred now," the man said.

They're talking about IV fluid. She rolled her head in response. Though she felt revived, she was not about to give these two her whole history right there while lying on the floor. Soon enough she'd have to face her suspicions from earlier that month.

And she couldn't blame Ash Meyers for this, could she? He of all people would know better.

~ ~ ~ ~

A woman having a miscarriage right in the middle of a raid? What a scene. You never knew when you undertook such an action what might unfold. And thank goodness for Helen Ramsey's presence, though her original scripted role bit the dust with this turn of events.

Agent Robert Cline stood at the front reception desk, cell in hand, barking orders to subordinates when necessary. They couldn't take the assorted others into the conference room with the doctor laying there bleeding, paramedics in attendance. The alternative – to sequester Chase Monroe and CEO Harris Vaughn in his private office until they completed their document seizure. And to detain a host of others separately for questioning as witnesses. Who knows? Perhaps several of them would later emerge as players. Other than Dr. Lange's situation, it had gone smoother than he'd expected.

At first blush, it appeared CEO Vaughn didn't know of the scheme Monroe had hatched, but he couldn't escape accountability. He was, after all, in charge of the entire nationwide operation. And how far and wide had these tactics spread?

Agents marched past periodically, conveying boxes of documents, laptops, desktop computer terminals to the waiting vans twenty stories down. Once they completed that task, he and several other agents would sit down with the major corporate figures and sort out the stories they'd tell. No doubt a score of attorneys would show up in the meantime. But first he would call for some lunch, fill their bellies but make them sweat a while longer, then commence the talking. He'd put the blond at the front desk to work on that. Order something which wouldn't make them sick to their stomachs. He'd had enough medical emergencies for one day.

Around the corner came the gurney bearing Dr. Erica Lange, two paramedics and Helen Ramsey bringing up the rear. Cline looked up from his cell and waved them to a stop, and took three steps to the side of the cart.

"Doctor, I hope you're feeling better soon," he said. Assessing her in the moment, he realized how pale and exhausted she appeared. He watched as a paramedic hung a second bag of fluid. And she probably needed more. Not a good situation.

She nodded in return.

He informed her, "I'll plan to speak with you later, when things settle down."

"We need to move on, sir, and get her to the hospital. She's still in pain, and needs attention right away."

Cline nodded. "Of course." Turning again to her, he added, "Take care." He watched as the paramedics hustled to the waiting elevator, propelling the gurney inside. The doors slid shut, and they disappeared.

Helen Ramsey remained there, leaning on the tall reception countertop, her normally placid face creased with worry lines. He immediately understood the look she threw him. Turning to Christy, he inquired of the lunch order processing, politely excused her from the front desk, and watched as she slunk away. No doubt she wondered where she could hide.

He turned to Helen. "Your impression?"

"She's got a big problem, there, miscarrying."

"She didn't know she was pregnant?"

"Didn't seem to, or is in denial."

"She's divorced, you know."

"No, I didn't. Only when you told me today."

"Has two other young kids from her first marriage." He paused. "Why do you think she showed up here today?"

"Most likely to confront the Monroe fella about the wrongful termination issue. And to let him know she had the goods on him. And whoever else he was working with at the facility in Kansas City."

Cline regarded Helen. "Sounds plausible. Looks like your conversations with her paid off. Did you encourage her to show up? Tell her about this plan?" He watched as Helen looked away, shook her head. He'd have to drill down there a bit further; that was obvious. But later. Let the dust settle a bit. He went on, "And what do you make of this other doctor she told you about?"

"Meyers?"

"Yeah, him."

"I'm not sure. I bet she has a thing for him, and was

145

disappointed or shunned, and decided to throw him under the bus while she was at it. I sure hope he's not the father of that baby."

He let her know, "He's married. Has two college-age sons. Do you think he's involved with the scheme?"

"Doubt it. He and his group attend at the facility, but there's no evidence so far that he's opposed to withdrawal of care, or there's no charting evidence to that effect."

The elevator doors opened and the delivery service approached the desk. Food had arrived. One less headache.

"Well, I appreciate all the work you've done, and coming all this way to help, Helen. I'd like you to hang around after lunch. We may need your input, and at least your presence from CMS may persuade our suspects that we're on to them."

The delivery man's eyes grew wide when he heard the word 'suspects', perhaps grasping then who stood before him.

Cline flashed him a smile, and withdrew a credit card from his pocket. It never hurt at such times for others to realize your true line of work.

TWENTY-SEVEN

November 1ˢᵗ

Friday

She gripped her abdomen where small bandages covered four tiny incisions. Her tender belly protruded. She didn't like her pregnant look, the equivalent of at least seven months gone. The pain was tolerable until she turned over or moved around, despite the narcotic they offered.

It had been a crappy night. Particularly after she'd returned from the OR. The constant stream of nurses traipsing in and out, completing their various duties, had made for interrupted sleep, no segment longer than one to one-and-a-half hours. Checking her vital signs, then a separate trip to adjust her IV, and another to monitor the packed red blood cell infusions she received, then to check her vaginal bleeding. To top it off, at around four thirty A.M. the lab tech appeared to draw the next scheduled bloodwork to check her anemia and the job the transfusions had done. And the Gyn had been right, despite Erica's assertions that perhaps she'd had a heavy late period or other source of pelvic bleeding. She had been pregnant, was suffering a complicated spontaneous abortion, had bled excessively, and required an urgent procedure. All in all, a horrid experience.

Her plan to be on a plane last night, winging her way home in time to see her kids wind up Halloween, was all shot to hell. What a mess. At least she'd been able to call sweet sister Susan late in the evening and fill her in, without telling too much. But, to be sure, she knew Susan then went to bed wondering how the hell that happened, and with whom she'd been consorting. There was a possible answer to that.

Erica heard voices outside her door. Within minutes the Obstetrician walked in – a kind, experienced, middle-age woman – with a staff nurse in tow. The poor lady doctor had been on ER call for Ob/Gyn the previous day and expected a busy night when they wheeled Erica in. They'd met briefly in the ER, then off to the OR – where she met anesthesia – then under she'd gone for the definitive intervention.

"How are you this morning, Dr. Lange?"

Erica struggled to prop herself up in bed. The nurse immediately came to her assistance, as the doctor looked on.

"Okay, I guess you'd say. Tired. Some pain…but only when I move."

The doctor nodded, chuckled, and moved to the bedside. She perched on the end of the bed, grew serious, and gazed at Erica. "You were very lucky."

"Was I?"

"I'd say so. It appears you lost close to a thousand from the bleeding, but we got in there quickly enough to stop it. Your hemoglobin was eight this morning. And your other lab is normal. You've had the three units of packed cells, which went well."

They stared at each other.

The OB went on, "You definitely had an ectopic, Erica, and we had to remove your right tube in the process. Your lab jived with your presumptive dates of about ten weeks. Of course, you'll need that rechecked in a couple of weeks along with following your crit."

"Right."

"We didn't find any other abnormalities when we looked around. Well, that tube was scarred but nothing else, and the left one looked normal."

"Good."

"After you receive the fourth unit of packed cells this morning, we'll wait six hours, and recheck another hemoglobin, hematocrit. If it's okay and your bleeding's slowed, we can dismiss you this evening. Do you have some place to stay overnight here in Chicago?"

"No, not other than the hotel, and I'd already checked out before this happened."

A frown creased the doctor's face. "Well, I don't like the sound of that. I think we can justify keeping you in until tomorrow morning, see how you're doing, then discharge you if everything's okay."

"Perhaps that's best."

"Here, let's take a look at your incisions." The OB rose, and examined Erica's abdomen and degree of bleeding. "Looks good. I hear bowel sounds. The bloat is from the laparoscope and the air, as you know, and will go down within a couple of days, a week at the most."

Erica nodded and dropped her head back on the pillow. The not-so-gentle exam had geared up her pain, left her feeling nauseous. Or that was the remaining vestiges of her pregnant state or the IV narcotics.

As she approached the door, the OB admonished, "Get up and around today, with assistance. It'll help things get back to normal. But make sure you're steady on your feet first." She turned to the nurse, and added, "We'll get her on a regular diet as tolerated, and take out her catheter, too."

Good news! Real food and no catheter. And some pain medicine, please.

She wanted to be more comfortable, and not sick to her stomach, when she placed the calls she needed to make. And find out where her wire went. Both her bra and it had disappeared, definitely not in her patient belongings bag. Best bet…either Helen Ramsey or that Agent Cline guy had it.

~ ~ ~ ~

"So, where are you?"

"Chicago."

"Chicago?"

Feinstein had been right, or their surveillance group had been right, when they followed her all the way to KCI and as far as her gate. And off she'd gone to corporate headquarters, but to do what? Put them on the spot, scream about her wrongful termination? No doubt, she'd done both.

She broke into his thoughts. "Yes. I went to corporate here to confront them about the whole scheme and my termination. Look them in the eye."

"And what did that produce?"

Ash leaned back in his desk chair for the duration of this hopefully brief conversation. He'd ignored her calls twice during hospital rounds that morning. But being efficient, he'd landed at his office by midafternoon to finish his week's work, and felt he should no longer avoid her repeated attempts to reach him. Besides, he wanted to know what the hell she was up to now. Keep an eye out, but keep his distance.

"Well, several things. They were shocked I'd come for one thing. And without realizing it, I walked right into an FBI raid on the company. And the woman from CMS showed up, too."

"That sounds like an active scene."

"Yes." She paused, then said, "It also produced an unexpected emergency."

What's the drama now? "What sort of emergency, Erica? That sounds like enough excitement for one day."

She cleared her throat, then he heard her speak to someone in the background about her tray and IV.

Where the hell is she?

As if reading his thoughts, she said, "I'm in the hospital, Ash, at Northwestern. Because…I, well, I suffered a ruptured ectopic yesterday in the midst of all that."

No way. He spun in his chair and leaned forward over his desk. "What? Are you okay?"

"Better. Stable now. I lost about a thousand. They gave me packed cells again this morning, then more observation. I'll probably leave tomorrow."

Stunned, he sat silent. *No way.* Why was she telling him this news? She could have waited until she returned home and things had settled down. And what interaction had she had with the FBI and the CMS woman while there? How did he play into all this?

"Ash, are you still there?"

"Yeah."

"Anyway, I just wanted you to know."

"Why, Erica, would I need to know?"

"Because, Ash, we had been together."

He waited, gathered his thoughts. She knew perfectly well – or should know – that ectopics don't rupture that early, before you even realize you're pregnant. Usually. And they'd consorted only two weeks ago...her timeline didn't fit. It usually takes at least eight or so weeks of fetal development to rupture the fallopian tube. At least that was his recollection from his one obstetrics' rotation in medical school. Granted that had been a long time ago, but he hadn't forgotten everything he'd learned in other specialties. What was she trying to pull?

"That's a little too soon for that, don't you think?"

"Perhaps..."

"At least the last time I consulted *Williams Obstetrics.*" Silence stretched between them. Disgusted, and a bit alarmed, he spoke first. "Look, Erica, I need to—"

"To get off, I know. But stranger things have happened, Ash, and I believe it's possible, since you're the only man I've been with in months."

"Stranger things have happened, I'm sure, but not in this case." He paused for effect, then informed her, "I've been fixed, Erica, a long time ago. I only shoot blanks."

TWENTY-EIGHT

Her eyes popped open and focused on the dim light seeping around the drapery edges. Was it cloudy or just too early yet? Margo lay still, wishing she could nod off again and ignore her thoughts, too many thoughts. Instead, she turned over, pulled her cell phone into view and squinted at the screen...5:50 A.M. Doubtful she could loll off given the night she'd had. And the night before that, and so on since Sunday.

The call from Ash, on Wednesday evening, had set her mind spinning. Dreading it, but at the same time relieved he'd tried twice to reach her, she'd hung up, not ready or able to handle her anger. He sounded truly repentant, she'd give him that. But it seemed the words had come too easily, not rehearsed, but too smooth. Admittedly, he'd always been good with words. Did he mean what he'd professed, or did he simply want his nice pat life put back in order? Neat and tidy, and her back home where he wanted her. Bottom line – how had he fallen so quickly for the advances of his conniving colleague? Was he really that gullible, that weak? She'd never thought that of her husband...he'd always seemed so strong. After all their years together...did she really know this man?

That is a very good question, girl!

Sleep abandoned, Margo sat and swung her legs over the edge of the bed. Stretching her back, she realized once again that neither of them had encountered such a creature before, that she could recollect. But still, he could have resisted, pushed back, persevered. And he had not. She rose and padded into the bathroom. It was time to prepare for another day, and to decide. Would she venture to Tulsa to check on progress there? The invitation she'd received earlier that week still hung out there, unanswered. He'd messaged her several times, not giving up so easily, certainly practicing good business follow up. And maybe something more? That thought brought a small smile.

It might just make for a good weekend getaway, after all.

Forty-five minutes later, after she'd showered, groomed and dressed, Margo prepared a fresh cup of coffee and made her way to the sitting area in her suite. A few new emails awaited: the shop verifying several fabric orders from earlier in the week, a dye lot had changed on another fabric – did she want to proceed? One associate had a sick child and wouldn't be in for several days, one lighting distributor could only fill part of an order and wanted an okay to send what they had. The remaining fixtures might be delayed six weeks. She could envision her client's reaction, and did not like what she saw. That one would take a soft, but firm, personal touch and negotiating to smooth things over. Or maybe she'd scrap the whole order and start over. Heavens! There was a lot to attend to.

Now the key question...was she going to Tulsa – escape, as it were – or stay put and handle the myriad of situations which had arisen overnight? She rose to refresh her coffee.

As she put her phone on the small refreshment bar, a Mozart piano sonata alerted her to an incoming call. Ignoring it for the moment, she focused on her coffee prep, and hoping it wasn't another design urgency, she debated whether to answer at all. Not a good idea, but it could wait – a little later would be fine. Finally Margo couldn't stand it any longer, and peeked at the screen, surprised at the caller ID.

No, really...why would he be calling?

TWENTY-NINE

Monday

Ash slumped in his office chair, exhausted. Waiting. The week had gotten off to a messy start at Oakwood, but he'd managed to get rounds done and things under control by midafternoon. Then he'd returned to his office to act busy until the appointed hour. June left him alone, unfortunately perhaps, to his own musings. He glanced at his watch. She would be there soon.

To say the weekend just past had dragged was an understatement. He'd moped around the house with Roberta all weekend, unshaven, not changing out of his flannels, hardly caring to eat regularly, exercise away his blues, or call his sons. His pal, she had reclined with him on the couch, consoled him with her paws and doleful looks of sympathy, had refrained from running around, and curtailed her dog smiling. She knew the score.

He hadn't reached Margo since their call the previous Wednesday evening. Was she in town somewhere or in Tulsa, or had she taken off for another destination? He could only imagine, and he fought his imaginings. Any thought of her elsewhere, still angry and fed up with him and his escapades, or interacting with some other charming man, was more than he could bear. He had to pull himself together, face the orchestra of discordant music he'd composed, and humble himself. The alternative was horrid.

Thank goodness he hadn't heard any more from Erica Lange, either. Most likely she was not in Chicago but back home, hopefully having come to her senses and tending to her children. The ones already on board and needing her. She was a smart woman, a good doctor, and needed to get herself straightened out, erase him from her radar screen, and move on. Last Friday afternoon she'd hung up rather abruptly after his announcement about his urologic reproductive adjustment. Whether she believed him or not was another matter.

At the sound of movement in the hall, he straightened in his seat, and closed down the hospital's homepage on his computer screen.

The door cracked open with June's help, and she informed him, "Your appointment is here."

"Good." He stood.

June leaned against the door, allowing entry for the expected person. "Ms. Helen Ramsey."

In walked the stout, middle-aged woman, about whom he had learned so much over the past three days. She wore a snug blue knit dress topped by a long jacket, and chunky-heeled navy dress shoes, which cupped her thick ankles. Shoes which provided stability. He restrained himself from his usual habit of assessing ankles for edema, and instead focused on her pleasant face and smile. Her carefully coiffed brown hair obviously hadn't given way, with the aid of hairspray, to the stiff Kansas 'breeze'. He tried to ignore the rather sizable red beaded necklace and earrings she wore. Floral perfume notes filled the air, which could prove a little hard to ignore if their anticipated discussion wore on.

He smiled, and introduced himself, then gestured, "Please, have a seat."

She glanced at both chairs and assumed the one directly

across from him as he resumed his desk chair.

"Please excuse me," he said, quickly texting the managing partner, requesting he put in an appearance in about twenty minutes. He muted his cell and placed it face down on his desk. She should appreciate his attempt to avoid interruptions during their important conversation.

He watched as Helen checked her phone one last time, also, and followed suit.

Momentarily, June tapped and stuck her head in the door, inquiring about any coffee, tea, or water they might desire. Both declining, she immediately shut the office door and retreated. A quick thought intruded that perhaps he should have concealed a bottle of bourbon in his briefcase that day, and the two of them might have gotten down to the honest truth quicker. Perish the thought of such an unlikely pair, sitting in a medical office, sloshing down whiskey on a Monday afternoon.

Refocusing then, he opened. "It's good to finally meet you, Ms. Ramsey. You requested the meeting, so perhaps you should start." Ash worked to maintain eye contact, and not study the bulging file folder she had deposited on his desk. Was he the subject of such a thick dossier already?

"Thank you for making time, Dr. Meyers. I know you're busy. Especially on a Monday." She finished with a smile. "I thought it was a good idea to come sooner rather than later and share information which we've accumulated at our CMS regional office. Then we can discuss your perspective. Perhaps finish with how this looks going forward."

Right. *Translation: you're in this for the long haul, buddy. Dismiss any thought you may harbor that this is coming to a swift conclusion.* He nodded, and motioned palms up. "Okay."

"So, as you may be aware, Dr. Erica Lange contacted our office two to three weeks ago. She reported the incidents involving herself and the staff at Oakwood Specialty Hospital, concerning withdrawal of care and DNR status. She referred to the situation there as a scheme and also informed us it was her belief she'd been fired due to her interference in the orchestrated plan. During the second call an individual from another federal agency was present while she reiterated the basic facts and freely named others who were involved in the scheme." Helen paused, and looking directly at him, said, "Your name was mentioned by Dr. Lange."

Schooling his expression, he sat silent.

"Were you aware of her naming you?"

"I have learned in recent days that she implicated me, yes." *To my wife in particular. And 'recent' can mean anything, right?*

"This is a serious matter, as I'm sure you're aware, Dr. Meyers. Do you have an answer to her allegations?"

"Yes. My answer – no, I'm not involved in some scheme, nor was I ever."

She studied his expression for a moment, then said, "Good." Why did he feel he'd just answered to his high school principal about a locker-room fracas and there were more questions to follow? "We wouldn't want to unjustly throw you into the basket of wrongdoers."

No, we wouldn't.

She shifted gears then. "About Oakwood Specialty, I understand you attend there from time to time. When was the last time you were there?"

"This morning."

Caught off guard, she registered surprise, regrouped, then said, "I see. So, you're still going there regularly?"

"Oh, yes, our group is. And I'm on this week. We rotate weekly, providing coverage there between our group members."

"Very well. At the present, they're remaining open, the facility, that is. The COO Kristine Nelson is gone, but an interim from one of their facilities elsewhere will serve as COO until a future appointment is made."

"I understood from her that she might seek a new position in another state. Do you know where she went?"

"I'm not at liberty to say, and I may have incomplete

information."

She slipped a piece of paper from her jacket pocket and slid it across his desk. On it was written the word, *Texas*. Ash gazed at her. *Is this woman wearing a wire?* He wouldn't doubt it, especially since they were apparently going to pass notes back and forth to each other. How untoward was this situation, anyway? She gave him a slight nod.

Okay, now he understood the rules of this game. "Of course," he agreed. "May I ask about the organization as a whole?"

"Yes. Go ahead."

"Is the corporation and their other facilities – are they going out of business any time soon?"

"We're not sure yet. That may happen at the conclusion of the investigation, but it's not happening in the near term."

"The CEO in Chicago is gone?"

"No. He is allowed to stay in place for now, provisionally, during the ongoing investigation. However, several other VP's have been appointed joint oversight." She paused. "But one VP there at the Chicago office has been suspended. He appears to have been involved in the plan, and is under investigation."

She did not volunteer the man's name, and Ash chose to let it go.

"I see. I understand the head of the internal medicine group at Oakwood who employed Dr. Lange has left." He scribbled Todd Griswold's name on the same slip of paper and slid it back toward her.

She nodded. "Yes. That's correct."

"Any others?"

"I believe the Director of Nursing is staying, but that may be contingent on several factors."

"Such as?"

"I'm not at liberty—"

"To say," he cut in. She responded to his interruption with a tight smile. Ash went on, "So, this brings us around to Dr. Lange again."

Helen said nothing, moved nothing.

"Would you care to share now what Dr. Lange told you about the scheme?" he asked. "I'd like to know if that squares with what she told me."

"Yes, I can," Helen said.

She launched into what sounded like a well-scripted narrative, describing Erica's two calls to her office and the details she'd shared of her experiences. And how she came to know of the nurses' and other staff's incentives for reporting her discussions with patients.

Ash listened intently, surprised actually that Helen's account jived with the discussions Erica had had with him, except her telling them he was involved, or at least, that he knew of the scheme. Helen confirmed to him that Erica had also admitted to calling the state hospital association, which had opened a parallel investigation.

When Helen concluded her reportage, Ash sat silent for a moment, then asked, "Will you tell me what exactly happened last Thursday when she showed up at the corporate offices in Chicago? She did call me after that to relay some of her unfortunate experience."

That seemed to reassure Helen that he wasn't simply fishing, though what he knew of Erica's gyn catastrophe he hadn't revealed. Nor, what he concluded her agenda had been for calling him.

"I was there, too. You know that the FBI conducted a planned raid on their offices. No advance notice given."

No, he hadn't known that, but now he did.

"Apparently, Dr. Lange had chosen that very day to show up, as well." Helen's expression appeared a bit strained.

Ash doubted the overlapping visits were a coincidence.

"At any rate, before too much time had passed, Agent Robert Cline came bustling down the hall with Dr. Lange on his arm. She, pale as a ghost. He brought her to the conference room and deposited her there. Before he could leave, she had sudden, severe abdominal pain and said she was bleeding. I helped her to the floor, and it was true. She was bleeding badly, miscarrying right there. Cline called the paramedics who arrived, stabilized her, then took her to the hospital."

"Northwestern, I believe."

Looking relieved he knew some detail, she said, "Right."

"Did she give much history? Was she stable enough to say much?" *Like how she implicated me as the father?*

"No, not really. She actually passed out initially and went down. The paramedics quickly started an IV, gave her fluid. She came to about five minutes later, wasn't really oriented, then seemed to improve somewhat. On her way out, she spoke with Agent Cline, then off they went. I inquired at the hospital, but they wouldn't release any information to me."

"Naturally," he added. "I do know she required emergency surgery that afternoon and had to be watched closely after that. That is some of the story she gave me."

But more information than that, he was not going to provide. It wasn't Helen Ramsey's business that Erica had an eight-to-ten-week pregnancy which ended in a ruptured ectopic, nearly costing her life. That was her story to tell. Which also meant to him that she made the rounds, had at least one other man tucked away somewhere, perhaps for whom another child would be an unexpected shock. He knew he couldn't be blamed for generating any of that.

She threw him a questioning look. He asked, "So, what is your take on her claims?"

"Well, we're in the midst of an investigation, which I've told you now involves the FBI. It may amount to a fraudulent scheme, a conspiracy to maintain high occupancy numbers, at times to the detriment of the patients and their families, and charging insurance and Medicare for expensive extra care. We do believe she has exposed a preplanned operation. Her termination simply opened it to scrutiny."

"Right. And if she'd let it go, didn't object to being fired, the whole thing might have continued for some time."

"Correct, Dr. Meyers."

161

"So do you consider her a whistleblower?" Or, were they working with and protecting Kristine Nelson as well? Had she also turned evidence for leniency? What an interesting mesh of players.

"Perhaps. But I can't confirm that at this time."

"Of course." He paused, then said, "I'm curious. Is the facility here the only one involved in this?"

"No. There is one other facility we know of, in Ohio, which is now also under investigation."

"Hum…"

A single rap on the door interrupted his thoughts. "Yes?"

Dr. Mitchell Burns eased the door open and waited for an invitation to enter. Ash nodded at him, and wasting no further time on formalities, Burns entered and closed the door. Ash stood, glad to peel himself from his chair for a few minutes, and glad for other company.

"Dr. Mitchell Burns, this is Helen Ramsey, from CMS."

Burns offered his hand, they shook, and he took the only remaining seat in the room. "Don't let me interrupt."

"No interruption. We were at a stopping point."

Helen jumped in, "It's very nice to meet you, Doctor."

"It's my pleasure, Ms. Ramsey."

Which Ash suspected it was not. But his partner was the consummate professional, both competent and always gracious and polite. So, it was assured no rudeness would intrude.

Introductions aside, Ash brought his partner up to speed on the conversation which had just elapsed, and the vital information regarding the ongoing function of the long-term acute care facility. It was critical for his group to know exactly how such a facility would run during a drawn-out investigation, and God forbid it should close, how they would disposition so many patients, some of whom still required ventilator respiratory support.

All three individuals, well, at least two of the three now involved in this discussion, knew that one does not quickly move such patients to another facility in town. Usually, only one such facility exists in a specified region, anyway. To add to the challenge, many long-term care units do not take patients on continued ventilator support, and that out-of-state arrangements are often the only solution. The stress for patients and families is overwhelming. To make sure Helen was up to speed on that issue, and mindful that their conversation may be recorded – for quality assurance purposes – Ash then asked Dr. Burns to state that. For the record. Which he did, succinctly.

Helen looked a bit surprised when he finished but nodded her understanding. Of course, to make sure she appeared on the ball about that, she clarified, "So, you're stating that a number of patients currently housed at Oakwood would require transport to facilities elsewhere, perhaps even out of state, where continued long-term ventilator management by qualified specialists could be provided? And that we at CMS, as well as their insurance companies, would have to approve such facilities?"

"That's exactly what we're saying, Ms. Ramsey. And such arrangements, should they become necessary, can take considerable time. Families often object to the move and spend much time finding places for their loved ones. And, frankly, may not be able to." Dr. Burns finished on a firm note.

"Oh. Yes, well, I understand. In that case, I believe that we at CMS may be able to provide support for such moves, if the patient has Medicare or Medicaid. And if the move is necessitated due to closure and our ongoing investigations."

"Very well, then," Burns said. "I'm satisfied that's understood." He pivoted toward Ash. "Ms. Ramsey, will you tell me, with Dr. Meyers present, how you see his involvement in this ordeal?"

How slick of him to put her on the spot. No 'he said, she said' later on. Ash relaxed a bit more. Burns was in his corner, or so it seemed at that point.

Appearing surprised at his directness, she answered, "Yes, I can." She shifted in her seat, then said, "Dr. Meyers has been very helpful today. It appears he will serve as an important witness to this whole process. I cannot see anything he's said here as an admission of purposeful involvement in this unfortunate scheme. And I do believe Dr. Lange told him things as this unfolded which affirm what she also told me."

She paused and looked at Ash. "However, I am concerned, Dr. Meyers, that she may have named you for personal reasons, and I feel it's only fair to warn you of my suspicions." She paused, then said, "To be blunt, if I may, I believe she has designs on your affections, if you know what I mean."

Boy, did he.

Burns reeled toward him, wearing a shocked look. It was clear there'd be some 'splainin' to do later.

Ash mustered an astonished expression and declared, "Well, that's a surprise." Though he could tell Helen, the mature woman she was, was having none of it.

"I'm surprised you weren't aware of her feelings. Well, at any rate, I think that can get ironed out as we go, but I felt the truth was of utmost importance between us."

And between you, your mic, and anyone else you see fit to share it with. Thank God none of this would be news to Margo, nor surprise her in the least. There was no naïve, uninformed spouse waiting at home. He'd already taken care of that from his end.

Dr. Burns' initial surprise subsided, he said, "Thank you for letting me in on that aspect of the situation, but I don't think, Ash, we need to share that with the entire group when we discuss the basic problem at Specialty and make our plans going forward."

"No, I don't think that needs to come up." Ash shot him a sharp look. *And please don't go home and tell Judy. Especially if she plans to order drapes from Margo.* "And I'm sorry you got dragged into that, Mitch. It is not a problem, I can assure you."

"Good, then." Burns glanced at his watch, and stood,

obviously ready to depart.

Ash knew his partner well. Burns would go home and think on this from every which way. And there were sure to be further conversations between the two of them.

Helen still seated, budged not. Ash was anxious to beat it out of there, too. It had been a very long day, and poor Roberta was waiting. As a signal, he arranged papers on his desk, then stood as well. Helen spoke before either man could make another move.

She ceremoniously glanced at her watch, then said, "There is someone I want you to meet, Dr. Meyers."

"All right. We can compare our calendars and set a time..." He glanced around at his desktop.

"That won't be necessary. They're here now." She pushed up from her chair, got her bearings, and moved to the door. Opening it, she smiled at the man who stepped forward and filled the door frame.

Turning toward the two doctors, she paused, then said, "Dr. Ash Meyers, this is Special Agent in Charge Robert Cline of the FBI field office here in Kansas City."

After that, Helen stepped aside as the tall, slender-framed man entered Ash's office and smiled.

"Agent Cline, Dr. Meyers. And this is his partner, Dr. Burns."

Ash shook Cline's offered hand and turned to his colleague. The look on Mitchell Burns' face – priceless. And it was not surprising at all when Burns could only manage, "FBI?"

Thirty

Dusk crept across the landscape. Exhausted, Ash drove slowly through the neighborhood and reached the end of his long drive. There'd been no real reason to hurry, other than Roberta's needs. The tall trees lining the one lane blacktop driveway reflected golds, reds, and browns in the long shadows of the setting sun. A few evergreens and blue spruce dotted their land, creating a brilliant color scheme.

Ash favored this time of year, when nature took over and turned their wooded lot into a picture-perfect Fall scene. Through the trees he could see a few windows, their bright lights beckoning. He must have left several on that morning to chase away the dark, or more likely he simply forgot to turn them off in his rush.

He turned into the drive, took a couple of curves, and slowed. About fifty yards away stood a woman on his driveway, cell phone in hand. God help him. Not Erica, surely? He stopped his SUV and stared through the dim early evening light. No, this was no raven-haired minx. This woman had lighter hair, obviously so in the dusky light. With it fastened back and swept up, she looked different. He eased forward and suddenly saw Roberta bound around the garage corner to her mistress and turn, alerting her to the approaching vehicle. Giving one bark, she ran up the drive toward him.

Margo looked up and smiled.

My God. He eased forward, not altogether assured this was what he'd hoped for. Had she simply returned to cart away more clothes and other personal belongings? She could have done that during the day and avoided him, unless she now sought another confrontation.

Nearer then, he killed the engine and climbed out. They stood apart for several moments, regarding each other in the receding light. God, it was good to see her. One week of separation had grown to months in his mind. Roberta bounded to the front door, signaling her understanding of this reunion.

"I…it's good to see you," he managed. Of course, it was.

"Yes. Yes, it is." She smiled and dipped her head.

Margo took one small step. Ash came unglued from his position, strode towards her, and wrapped her in his arms. She felt so good to hold, he was not at all inclined to let go. Or ever hold any other woman. This was where he belonged. How close he'd come to losing her.

"I don't want to let go. I missed you…"

A shiver ran through her body, softly vibrating her frame against his. "Scott called me." She waited, then eased back a bit and gazed at him. "Let's go inside. It's a bit chilly out here."

He smiled and planted a firm kiss on her forehead. Securing an arm around her waist, he propelled her toward the front porch. "Fine with me."

Roberta wagged and waited at the door, her smile restored.

"How did your day go?" Margo asked.

Her usual question engendered a deep, warm well of emotion. The comfortable familiarity he longed for, so often previously taken for granted until nearly lost. As they climbed the brick porch steps, a surprising sense of peace and comfort settled over him.

"You're not going to believe what you're about to hear."

"Try me."

THIRTY-ONE

November 11th

Monday

She wiggled into the cowl-neck black tunic, grey plaid slacks, and found the black flats she'd chosen. And she pulled her hair back and up again in a twist, getting the mane under control. Surveying herself in the mirror, she found her appearance satisfactory. This appointment had to go well. Her future depended on it...pretty much.

Erica had scurried around early that morning, preparing the kids for school, running the necessary route to and from, then had settled in at home and calmly prepared. The agreed upon meeting time was set for ten A.M. It had been almost ten days since she'd left Northwestern Medical Center, sufficiently stable, and had flown home. Thankfully, due to her sister's efforts, her kids hadn't missed a beat, loved visiting their aunt, uncle, and cousin, and were full of tales of Halloween escapades. Their impression – mommy got sick while at her medical meeting and couldn't get home when expected. Oh, well. And the intervening week of 'normalcy' had passed without further incident on anyone's part. Now, here she stood. Ready.

~ ~ ~ ~

"Please come in, Dr. Lange…do have a seat."
Helen Ramsey indicated a comfortable-appearing upholstered chair positioned opposite hers across a round table. No corners to negotiate. One could reposition, at will, during an ensuing interview to effect a more confidential exchange if desired. A very effective arrangement, which was not lost on Erica.

They were the only two people in the small conference room at the regional CMS office in Kansas City. It was straight up ten o'clock as scheduled. Erica's assessment of the setting did not require much time before she took her seat.

The room boasted neutral office décor, recently updated to reflect the soft greys and beiges so typical of government facilities these days, and gave off a modern vibe. The geometric-patterned carpet – produced with carpet tiles arranged in somewhat haphazard manner – delivered its own design message. Perhaps meant to achieve an unstructured look and imply that free-form thought might surface in such a place. An offset to the very structured activities which chugged along in such bureaucratic offices. More likely and more importantly, it served a very practical purpose when a nasty coffee or food stain called for a quick tile replacement.

Natural light streamed in through high-set lateral windows abutting the false ceiling, positioned to eliminate the need for blinds to assure privacy. But, which also prevented gazing out of windows as one collected one's thoughts during a discussion. No, one would need to maintain eye contact, or gaze at nondescript landscape prints which graced two of the walls. The set-up was perfect for the business at hand.

"Thank you."
Helen offered and dispensed coffee from a rather elaborate machine positioned and ready on an adjacent

countertop. In fact, that whole wall was taken up by grey laminated built-ins, primarily bookshelves with cabinets beneath, loaded with official-appearing publications from HHS and other pertinent divisions of the federal government. The monikers on their spines left no doubt as to their origins. This apparently served as a library of sorts for certain personnel lucky enough to possess the door code. Employees did not come in there for a quick coffee break or to consume their sack lunch, no sir, unless they wished to peruse the Federal Register.

Seated again, Helen sipped then spoke. "So, I hope you've been well."

"Yes, I'm feeling much better. Thank you."

Helen smiled. "And your children are fine?"

"Yes, quite well. Busy at school."

Helen nodded. She was obviously waiting, killing time before getting underway. Was an expected someone else late in arriving? Was the plan to confront her with Dr. Ash Meyers again, or perhaps some unlucky devil from Oakwood? Erica was not about to jump in and rush this process.

A few more moments of chit chat passed when they both heard a clicking at the door, and turned in that direction. As the door swung open, Erica was not at all surprised. She'd been wondering for over a week when this conversation would finally take place and now it was at hand. A look of relief swept over Helen's face. Special Agent Robert Cline had arrived.

THIRTY-TWO

He approached the table with a broad smile, offered a friendly hand, and carefully chose one of the remaining two chairs, pushing the other off to the side. More room to maneuver when one wished to align with a particular discussant. Erica returned his friendly greeting and waited.

After folding his tall frame into the rather low chair, he said, "I trust you're doing well, Dr. Lange."

"Yes, thank you."

"I'm sorry for your loss, and the urgency it created for you in Chicago. Please accept my sympathies."

"That's kind. Thank you."

He regarded her for a moment, then began. "We asked you to come in today to begin discussion about the unusual situation you found yourself in over the past month or so. Before we proceed further, I need to make it clear you may invite legal counsel to join these discussions if you desire. Have you been made aware of that?"

"Yes, I have."

"To be clear, I am not taking an official statement from you today, not anything of the sort, but what you say may

172

impact how you proceed later, and what your testimony may entail later. Is that clear to you?"

"Yes."

"Good. And your choice was to come alone today to meet with us?"

"Yes." He was going on a bit too much, though. Now she wondered, sitting there with the two of them...perhaps she should have invited some company? Oh, well.

He nodded agreement as well, and continued, "As I'm sure you know, we've investigated the organization, Oakwood Specialty Hospitals, Inc., concerned about irregularities in their operation. And that certain individuals within the organization have allegedly colluded or conspired to gain from inappropriate policies involving medical care at several of their facilities. This is particularly of interest to us if it involved Medicare, Medicaid, or insurance billings suggestive of possible fraud."

He paused and leaned back in his chair. "It appears your employment there and your position on such medical cases accelerated this coming to our attention. Fortuitous, you might say."

Erica nodded, maintaining an even expression.

"One question I have. Is it correct to say you knew nothing of this scenario when you joined the internal medicine group Premier Medical Associates four months prior?"

"That's correct, Agent Cline. Nothing."

"Okay. I understand you signed a formal employment agreement with that medicine group, standard contract such as that."

"Yes, I did. On June first."

He smiled, then asked, "You received what you would consider a proper orientation to the position when you hired on, both from the chief of the internal medicine group Dr. Todd Griswold, and the COO Kristine Nelson. They outlined the concept of long-term acute care, and the policies of the institution, correct?"

"Yes, that's correct. Actually, more than once."

"Oh?" He paused, apparently reconsidered, then said, "We can go into that a little later. So, tell me, did you receive a written policy manual?"

"No, actually I did not."

"All right. And you became aware of some activities through your own observations, and those of several others, including your group's nurse practitioner. Is that correct?"

"Yes, that's right. And several other staff nurses."

"Okay. Why don't you tell us about those observations?"

"Certainly."

Erica took a deep breath, sipped her cooling coffee, and began. She succinctly outlined her initial experience at Oakwood, her concern for the patients and their clinical course before admission to the facility, and their prospect for recovery. She described her position on excessive resuscitation efforts, often not desired nor appropriate for their various conditions, in her opinion.

After her prelude, she dove into specific occasions when she realized she had been reported to the Director of Nursing or Dr. Griswold for seeking a 'no code' status from a patient and family. Nurses documenting her conversations with patients, which were reported as complaints from patient's families, as well as 'counseling' or reminder comments from her colleague Dr. Griswold regarding long-term acute care and its purpose.

Cline remained impassive as she narrated, but visibly alerted when she next broached the subject of favorable treatment and incentives extended to such staff members.

How had she specifically found out about those arrangements? he asked.

Through conversations overheard by the nurse practitioner Raina Crawford, she explained, and other disenchanted staff not included in the scheme.

That held Cline's attention. He asked her and she obliged with various specific instances she could recall of 'spying', his eyes narrowing a fraction at her words, her only clue of his particular interest in that aspect of the case. Finished, Erica sat back and waited for his next volley of questions.

Assuming a thoughtful expression, Cline regarded the table and gazed at the far wall before revealing any considerations. Sitting forward then, he leaned on the table and looked at her.

"We appreciate your candor. As you may realize, this is a complicated process now underway, and will take time to unravel, though I suspect not as long as I at first expected. Since you were present, you're aware perhaps – though you were indisposed at the time – that we confiscated documents and electronically stored data for our investigation. At any rate, we did, and are now reviewing those we have in our possession. Following that and with the help of CMS, and Ms. Ramsey, we'll want to interview you again."

He smiled, and went on. "We consider you, at this point, an important witness to this process. I don't know if you understand you are, in fact, in the position of being a whistleblower. And that can bring its own challenges."

Erica nodded.

"And there are others, of course. Witnesses."

"Yes."

"So, we wish to keep you and your children safe while this process unfolds, and perhaps afterwards."

Is he talking witness protection? Her heart pounded. She reached for a quick sip of now cold coffee. It was time to start asking some questions of her own.

Apparently sensing her distress, Helen got to her feet, and said, "Here, let me warm your coffee."

"Safe? What are we talking about here?"

"Yes. As you know, we provide services, a program for valuable witnesses in certain cases. This has not risen to that level yet, though we are monitoring the situation. So, at this time we don't recommend that to you. But, if our level of concern changes or as this expands, we may need to readdress that option."

With the steaming new cup in hand, Erica took a

welcome sip and tried to relax. "I see."

"In the meantime, we'd like to offer you and your family protection through lower-level surveillance, activities such as that."

"I don't want a constant tail, or phone tapping, if that's what you're referring to. But I would welcome some protective detail, especially where my children are concerned."

"We are fine with that, and I think you'll find that not too intrusive. They fade into the background fairly well. But can mobilize quite quickly if the need arises."

"One thing you said earlier about *others,* witnesses that is…who are you referring to?"

"I can't reveal names right now, but there are other individuals who were involved in this situation who may serve in the same capacity as yourself, you understand that."

Kristine Nelson? Ric Newman? Had the latter two turned evidence to save their asses? She wouldn't doubt it.

"I have another question, then. As I'm sure you know, I wore a recording device that day to the Chicago headquarters, thinking I would get Chase Monroe to say something I could use against him. Where did that go? And my bra. It was not in my belongings when I came back from surgery that Thursday evening."

Agent Cline smiled. "We have that. And it's proved quite useful up to this point."

"So, I won't get the recording back?"

"Not now, no. If you need it in the future for any legal proceeding, we can provide that to you and your counsel."

"Okay, as long as I can retain the right to have access."

Impassive, he nodded.

"You know, I may still pursue the wrongful termination complaint against the company."

"We understand that. If there's a company left to pursue."

Good point.

Helen shot Cline a look, a signal perhaps to change gear.

"Speaking of which, what are your thoughts, your plans, for your future medical practice?"

Erica divided a quick look between them. There was suddenly something quite orchestrated about the turn of conversation.

"I've received an opportunity to consider aesthetics, going into outpatient practice with a residency friend who has started such a clinic in St. Louis. Since I hold a Missouri license the move from a practice standpoint would be somewhat easier, and I have family there. So, help with the children would also be a huge benefit. I don't see anything holding me here, so it's something I've been considering."

Cline smiled and nodded. "Sounds like you've been doing some serious thinking in a rather short time."

"Yes, I have. Crises can accelerate decision-making, I've found."

"Certainly. Well, I'm glad to hear you feel positive about your options."

He turned to Helen. "I believe it's time for me to leave. This has been a productive conversation, Doctor, and I look forward to further interviews in the future. And I want you and Ms. Ramsey to stay in contact, as well. So, I'll be off."

He pushed up from his chair, stretched briefly, and strode toward the door. No reason to tarry.

"I'll talk with you both later." With a smile, and a knowing look thrown to Helen, he left, closing the door almost silently.

THIRTY-THREE

M s. Ramsey did not rise, nor give any signal their meeting had concluded. A sudden thought intruded, as she and Helen sat quiet, exchanging pleasant smiles. What did Helen Ramsey and Robert Cline already know of her new opportunity? Was her residency pal suddenly interested in another associate, or had the Bureau stimulated and orchestrated that whole idea? Was this, in fact, a modified witness protection maneuver?

It was likely best to avoid such analysis, at least at the present time.

Momentarily, Helen inquired again about beverages. While she performed her hostess duties, Erica checked her watch. All of that covered in only about thirty minutes. They had time to burn. And more curious then, Erica waited.

Helen resettled herself, ready to go on. "I just want to let you know how concerned I've been about your situation there in Chicago. I'm aware you lost your baby, and went through quite an ordeal in the process."

"Yes, I had an ectopic pregnancy, as it turns out."

"My…yes, well, of course…"

"And the surgery went well, and I'm recovering as expected. I do appreciate your concern. Thank you."

Helen lowered her head momentarily, then looked at Erica and said, "I've had some personal experience with pregnancy loss myself. I had one daughter, then suffered three miscarriages after that. Never had another child." Her eyes misting, she added, "So, I know how that goes."

Instinctively, Erica touched her arm. "I'm sorry to hear that. It doesn't leave you, does it?"

"No, never." Helen composed herself, smiled briefly, and asked, "So, you have support if you move to St. Louis? Your folks?"

Erica straightened and said, "Well, my father lives there with his second wife. My mother died of breast cancer when I was only twenty. She was obviously rather young when she passed."

"Oh, my, hon. I am sorry to hear that." With a maternal gesture she warmly grasped Erica's hand. "You have been through a lot."

"Some would say so. And I believe those experiences colored my thinking about the whole issue at Oakwood."

"My, yes. I can see that." Helen shifted in her seat, and they released their grasp of each other. It was obvious she hadn't said all she desired. "So, Dr. Ash Meyers you worked with..."

Here it is.

"Have you spoken with him since your return?"

"No, no I haven't."

Helen smiled, apparently relieved she'd finally spoken the words. "How do you see him, where does he fit into the picture?"

Erica smiled. "I like your directness, Helen. In a word, nowhere, really."

"I had some concern...that you..."

"I understand. You were concerned I had pursued him, that maybe the baby was his?"

"Yes, well, you know..."

179

"It wasn't, and I don't have designs on him. So, that – the pregnancy – was the product of another recent relationship gone bad, and the outcome was probably for the best, hard as that is to say. Sometimes circumstances shake us up, don't they, and for good reason. And that can prove positive, in the end."

"Yes, it can."

It felt good to unload. Erica went on, "Frankly, I'm ashamed I chased him for his help with the situation. I believe I rather lost my mind for a short time, stressing over the issue at the facility. And the suspicion I was pregnant. I tried to find safety and solace anywhere I could. And he was handy, seemed sympathetic…and is more than attractive."

"That he is," Helen agreed with a sly smile.

Goodness, what about this bonding!

After a pause, Helen pushed her chair back. "I won't keep you any longer. Sounds like you have many things to attend to." She rose and took her mug to the sink.

Erica followed suit, glad to be on her feet again and move around. Her days now were interrupted by sudden periods of profound fatigue, which she knew would plague her for some weeks to come. It was time to go home and rest before picking up her kids at school.

Near the counter the two women paused, and on an impulse, Helen wrapped Erica in a warm hug. The stout woman embracing her in such a maternal gesture of care, Erica felt the pang of a mother lost, the closeness she'd not enjoyed for many years suddenly surging.

She pulled back after a moment, gazed at the watery brown eyes – kind eyes – and took hold of Helen's arms in a firm clasp.

"You're too kind." She returned the hug. "Thank you."

"You take care of yourself, you hear?"

"You bet. How could I do otherwise?"

EPILOGUE

December 2nd

Monday

The Monday after Thanksgiving weekend always proved hectic. Consults and admissions from the weekend required close follow-up to make sure their workup was completed or at least underway, and that appropriate treatments had been implemented by the pared-down holiday staff. It was his least favorite Monday of the year. And it was his turn at Oakwood. Ahead lay a full week for sure.

The few dialysis patients settled in and underway, Ash rounded the corner of the east wing. Making a quick pivot, he barely avoided running into Ric Newman.

The Director of Nursing apologized for tearing around half-cocked. It had been a busy morning for him, too.

"How's it going?" Ash asked.

"Not the best. We're short again." Newman said no more and changed course, heading in the opposite direction once again.

Preoccupied, Meyers opened the computer cabinet at a nearby patient's door. "I'm sorry to hear that. We've got a lot to get done this week."

"Right," Ric called back over his shoulder. After apparently a moment's consideration, he stopped and returned to the nephrologist. "Got a minute?"

Ash looked up from the electronic record. "Sure."

181

Impressed by the nurse's serious expression, he ceased his chart review and paid attention.

Ric took a step and closed the adjacent patient's door, then glanced up and down the hall before speaking again. Ash found himself checking the hall, both directions, as well. Can't be too careful. *And whatever he's got on his mind must be important.*

"So, I've wondered how that whole thing with Dr. Lange ended up."

Ash searched Ric's face before rushing to answer. *Too much information, not a good idea. What did he already know?* "I believe it's ongoing, the investigation, if that's what you mean. I heard somewhere she moved to St. Louis, closer to family, I guess."

Ric nodded. "She doesn't stay in touch with you?"

"No...no."

Ric assumed a broad-based stance and crossed his arms, protecting his mid-section. A body posture not lost on Ash. "Dr. Meyers...I want you to know, I became aware of that plan they all hatched very late in the game. And I was uncomfortable from the get-go reporting on a doctor. Towards the end, I gave them bits of information, but not anything damning. Nothing that made any difference, I don't think."

"Have the authorities spoken with you?"

"On one occasion. That's all. And they didn't seem too interested in what I had to say."

"That's probably a good sign. And you probably shouldn't tell me anything else. Better if I don't know any of your particulars." He smiled at Ric and saw his face relax, his jaw clenching ceased. "Looks like you held onto your position. One of only a few."

Ric returned his smile. "Yeah, so far."

"I'm glad you didn't get washed away in the tsunami."

"I am, too." Checking the halls again, Ric assumed a low tone, "You know, it's been different around here, though, since Dr. Lange left."

"Oh?"

"Yeah, not as good. We miss her."

Ash gazed at the man and smiled.

"I meant, she's a good doctor, and I agreed with her assessment of the patients, her perspective. She did a fine job for them."

"Yes, I believe she did."

"I've heard that several new internists will start soon. Any chance, you think, she might return?"

"We got wind of that, too...the new people coming on board. But no, I seriously doubt that Dr. Lange will be back."

Ric nodded, then added, "Well, I want you to know, we hope your group stays on. You all deliver quality care, and we need that here especially with this upheaval and all. Please let me know if you notice anything which needs addressing."

"You bet."

As Ric turned away, Ash recalled the younger man's situation, and said, "When's that wedding?"

Ric turned and grinned. "May, if all goes well. Keep an eye out for a 'save-the-date' in the mail before too long."

"Thanks, I wouldn't miss it. And it will go well...all of this. We'll make sure of that."

AUTHOR'S NOTE

Long-term acute care, or LTAC for short, is a medical care model familiar to few, usually only those whose family member has required extended intensive care, often after a rather complicated hospital course. But they have stabilized and show a propensity for recovery. Not to be confused with other long-term care facilities, such as nursing homes, at an LTAC facility a patient must make steady progress to a proposed discharge date, usually within ninety days, though some do remain longer. Developed in part when hospitals reduced length of stay for all sorts of diagnoses, this model of care has gained traction across the country in recent years.

So much for the lecture. It is a very challenging medical setting, and the doctors and nurses who choose to work there provide excellent care for such patients.

But please remember, this particular story is all fiction. Though I'm familiar with such a setting, these characters are not individuals I have known or worked with. Also, I seem to enjoy involving the FBI in my stories, and again, if my depictions are inaccurate, I assume all responsibility for such lapses.

Thanks to my editor Laura Taylor for her diligent work, providing invaluable suggestions and corrections along the way. Kudos also to Sharon Kizziah-Holmes and Jaycee DeLorenzo for their formatting and graphic design expertise. And to all for their patience, wisdom, and humor during the sometimes-tedious process of book preparation and production.

As always, a big thank you to my husband for his encouragement and steady support. He and his colleagues are some of those physicians who have labored long hours to serve patients and their families such as those depicted here.

I enjoyed bringing these conflicted characters to the page, and wrestling with their shortcomings and ultimately their renewed strength. Hopefully, you found PROSCRIPTION enlightening, and at least a little entertaining, and I very much appreciate you sharing your time.

JJ Renek

September 2025

About the Author

JJ Renek is the pen name of retired physician Dr. Janna Trombold.

Pivoting from a major in English literature, she pursued a career in obstetric nursing, and holds both a BSN and MSN in that field. A decade and two children later, she returned to medical school and received her MD from the University of Texas Southwestern Medical School in Dallas. During that time, she collaborated on several creative projects including faculty roasts and writing for the annual, irreverent senior video produced, in turn, by her medical school class.

Since retiring, she has penned eight medical suspense novels, and a collection of short stories across various genres. JJ makes her home with her husband, minus any wild pets, in the 'Show-Me State' where she writes full-time.

You can follow JJ on Bookbub, Amazon, or Facebook at jjrenekauthor. Or to learn more about her and her books, visit her website at: www.jjrenek.com. While there, you can join her newsletter group to receive updates and stay in the loop.